POOR LITTLE MIXED GIRL

THE MIXED GIRL SERIES BOOK ONE

LAMONIQUE MAC

POOR LITTLE
MIXED GIRL

For every orphan who's ever been treated like they were one.

ALSO BY LAMONIQUE MAC

The Mixed Girl Series
Poor Little Mixed Girl (Book One)
Mixed Out (Book Two)
Snakes in the Mix (Book Three)

Ubiquitous Ministries
Overcoming Anxiety in the Hood

SIGN UP FOR MY AUTHOR NEWSLETTER

Be the first to learn about LaMonique Mac's new releases and receive exclusive content for fiction readers.

CONTENTS

1. East vs. West   1
2. Friends Ready? Okay!   7
3. Ms. Eleanor   17
4. The Tennant   26
5. The Babysitter   37
6. The Pursuit of Freedom   46
7. LaMonica With "the Good Hair"   55
8. A Time to Explode   61
9. Little Ms. Mexicana   66
10. The Three Amigos   71
11. He Ain't "Crazy" in Love   83
12. School Daze   88
13. Attic Antics   99
14. "Real" Family   108
15. Now Everybody's Getting Tipsy   120
16. Oklahoma Is Not OK!   125
17. The Queen Meets the Bishop   135
18. Culture Shock   143
19. The Bishop Makes His Move   151
20. Chester, Chester   157
21. Runaway Child   167
22. The Plan   173
23. Good Deals Gone Bad   181
24. The Proposal   190
25. The Final Test   197

Newsletter Signup   215
Thank You   217
Acknowledgments   219
About the Author   221

1

EAST VS. WEST

Mama was putting the pedal to the metal, trying to get LaMonica across the city and to school on time. LaMonica was in her last year at Kempton Elementary near the suburbs of Saginaw, and even though the little city was small, fighting the morning traffic could be hectic.

Of course she didn't make it easy, dilly dallying and "playing around" every morning, when it was time to get ready for school.

For the life of her, Mama couldn't understand why LaMonica found it so hard to stay focused.

She would start putting on a shirt, then run to the bathroom and dance around while brushing her teeth. Then she would remember that she still wanted something off her plate from breakfast that morning and run into the kitchen and eat that.

Mama would be ironing her work clothes and yelling, "LaMonica, are you almost dressed?"

"Um no, I can't find my pants Mama. Oh wait, I found them. Now I can't find my shoes."

"LaMonica, I swear you would forget where your head was if it wasn't attached to yo' body."

Ella Mae Powers absolutely refused to be a parent who got her child to school late. She believed in an on time God, and she was an on time representative. *We've already had a late start because of LaMonica. Now all these doggone cars are in the way.*

"I have to fight traffic every morning tryin' to take you to school on time," Mama said.

"Just look at all these cars coming from the west side over here to the east side. All these peckerwoods taking all the jobs from folks on the east side of the city.

"I can't have no job in the plant like they can, but these peckerwoods can come over here on our part of town and make all the money."

Mama often remarked how she doesn't like that Whites come over to "her" side of the city and take all the good jobs.

This thinking is ironic because Mama and LaMonica travel every day to the west side, which is considered "the White part of town" in order for her to reach school.

Ever since Kindergarten there had only been three Black children in LaMonica's grade. And only five Black children besides herself attended the entire school.

There was a mixed girl there named Monica who LaMonica had become classroom friends with. Monica's mother was Mexican, and her father was biracial (Black and White). Her skin looked White, but her auburn afro hair told a different story. You could tell she wasn't White, but she wasn't exactly Black either. LaMonica would later learn in life that with race, the saying goes, "If you have to ask, then they're Black."

LaMonica was often one of those who had to be *asked*. She had always considered herself Black. Although the kids in her neighborhood **did** let her know she was different. She was used to seeing lots of brown skinned Black people all around her as a part of her neighborhood community - First Ward Community Center, Mt. Olive Church, everywhere. So being one of the three Black children in a class of twenty-five was a bit different.

Out of the twenty-five children in Mrs. Meijer's class the Black children comprised of Derick, Gillette and herself. Even though LaMonica was mixed with both Black and White, she hadn't been taught that. As far as she understood things she was Black. Mama was brown skinned and Black, and her brother Richard was brown skinned and Black too. All the pictures she had seen of her sister Deb were of a brown skinned Black person as well.

Based upon LaMonica's looks, most of the children in her community let her know she *was* different. She wasn't always accepted as being Black. But here at school it was obvious everyone from the teacher to the principal to the school aides and all the children - saw her as Black. She was Black from within her soul. LaMonica unwittingly carried her community's culture with her everywhere she went. She exuded blackness from her verbiage to her neck rolls and attitude swag. Culturally, she was Black and marked at school from day one.

Not only was LaMonica culturally Black but socio-economically she was from the east side. Upon attending Kempton Elementary, she would learn she came from the lower class of town. All of the other students lived near the suburbs, and that's why they went to school at Kempton.

Mrs. Powers (LaMonica's mother) was the only parent

that year to take part in open enrollment. A program for parents to choose a school outside of their neighborhood district for a student to attend.

The other Black children in the school had parents who worked in the GM Plant and made good money. They could never imagine what it was like to live in a neighborhood on the north-east side, like 5th and Kirk. In the 80s, it was more like living in the wild, wild west.

LaMonica would rather just attend school on the east side with the kids that lived in her own neighborhood. Obviously she didn't fit in at this suburban school, and these rides to the west side were frustrating for Mama every morning.

"Mama, why do I have to go to school so far away? I wanna go to Longstreet like the other kids in the neighborhood," LaMonica whined.

"Girl, I know you ain't gettin' mouthy with me this morning!"

There wasn't a formal question to the words Mama was saying, but LaMonica knew that tone and she'd better answer it quick and with respect.

"No, ma'am I'm sorry Mama."

"And another thang when you go to school today, I don't want to hear no bad reports about you, LaMonica. Your school work is important. Friends don't mean nothin'. So don't be talking in class and not getting yo' lesson."

Ah man, LaMonica knew she had gotten her mama started now. *If only I hadn't said anything about wanting to go to Longstreet, I wouldn't have gotten Mama started.* Whenever Mama or others LaMonica knew who were originally from down south got upset their English became more and more broken with a mix of southern and hood.

On the ride to Kempton, Mama continued reminding

her it was important to get her lesson and to stay out of trouble. LaMonica knew the most important thing ever is to **never** embarrass Mama or the family. Although she rarely did the best job at that one.

She also knew that whenever she wanted Mama to say, "yes" to something, it was best to speak in a baby voice. This would also ensure she wasn't mistaken for "talking with an attitude" which was high on the list of sins a Black child had better not do!

In a sweet baby voice LaMonica said, "Mama, can I stay after school for cheerleading tryouts?"

"Cheerleading tryouts? How much is that?"

"Nothin' Mama, it's free."

"Ain't nothin' free. Don't you have to buy uniforms?"

Mrs. Powers was a widow, raising LaMonica alone. She simply didn't have extra funds for things that weren't necessary.

"Yes, but they said we can sell candy to pay for them."

"Okay. I'll pick you up an hour after school." Mrs. Powers said as they entered the drop off point at Kempton Elementary.

"Thank you, Mama. Bye."

"Bye. Now have a good day. And don't get in trouble."

They made it to school when all the other students were standing outside, so everybody had seen LaMonica get dropped off in the front. She already knew this meant the kids were going to tease her about her car again.

In 1987 Mama drove a 1972 Monte Carlo. When LaMonica first started school at Kempton, she had no idea how different her car was from the other kids' families' cars. Being not a detailed person, these sorts of things usually slipped by her. Some kids from school that day were sure to point it out to her, though.

LaMonica determined today she wouldn't get in trouble. If Derick Johnson or Emily Wolfe teased her about her car, she would fight hard to ignore it. She wouldn't do anything to jeopardize being able to try out for cheerleading after school.

2

FRIENDS READY? OKAY!

Somehow LaMonica managed not to get into "her usual trouble" in class, which was a stipulation for anyone trying out for the cheerleading squad.

The bell rang, and she made her way down the halls to the cafeteria with excitement. LaMonica and Monica were still friendly with each other, but they had grown apart through the years, likely a warning from her mother to not become too involved with "the school problem child." LaMonica asked her if she was interested in trying out for the cheerleading squad with her. Monica declined. So she realized she would have no allies once she made it there.

No quite the opposite. Emily Wolfe was sure to be present and accounted for and most likely picked for the cheerleading team. With her training in ballet, tap, and jazz she was a shoe in.

LaMonica had once asked Mama if she could take tap and ballet like Emily.

Mama responded, "Ain't nobody got no money for that."

"And besides, they work them girls until they cry and their toes bleed. You don't want that LaMonica."

Once money was mentioned LaMonica should have known it was out of the question. Still, she dreamed of being good at something like tap. Ever since Emily had bragged about it to her at school, she had begun watching Sammy Davis Jr. on TV and putting on her patent leather church shoes (they looked almost like tap shoes). She even began wearing them to school with her jeans and tapping down the halls. Which she was often reprimanded for.

At lunchtime, when she was often in time out (with all the other children who couldn't follow the rules) and had to stand in the gym's corner, she would tap with her church shoes, like she knew what she was doing.

After daydreaming, LaMonica finally arrived at the cafeteria. Everyone else was already there. She was late. Because she often got lost in her thoughts, she was often late for class or anything where Mama wasn't right by her side to escort her to.

All the girls trying out for cheerleading were so pretty. Emily was there among them. Her honey blond hair swinging as she practiced her twirls from ballet, waiting on cheer practice to officially begin.

Kempton was lucky. Some varsity cheerleaders from Arthur Hill High School had come over to teach the 6th graders cheers. There was a mix of blond and brunettes with slinky figures.

LaMonica raced in and lined up just in time to get started.

"Hi. My name is Brook, this is Sheila, Heather, and Becky."

"Being a cheerleader is important to your school's spirit," Brook explained.

"Yes! It's your movements and enthusiasm that can help

spur your team on to victory," Heather enthusiastically exclaimed.

"Today we will show you some of our cheers. We will judge you based on how well you can follow directions and keep pace with the group. Good luck ladies," Becky offered.

"Get ready for cheer one."

"We are the Cougars; We can't be beat.
Because we've got the power to knock you off your feet.
Boom, boom, boom, boom."

OKAY. I like this beat. This song is easy, LaMonica thought to herself.

Team leader Sheila stepped in front.

"Okay ladies, now it's time to add in these simple cheer steps," Sheila instructed.

Sheila began doing what she claimed were simple cheer steps, but LaMonica just couldn't seem to catch up. When she managed to get one move right it was out of time to the rhythm of the cheer.

They kept taking the time to re-instruct her. She would feel like she was keeping up with the rest of the girls, but the feedback from the cheer team leaders and Emily Wolfe said otherwise.

This same scenario played out with every cheer she tried. LaMonica just knew in her heart if she had more than just this one day to be judged, she could eventually learn what they were teaching. Although Mama had always told her she was clumsy, so maybe not.

Cheer practice ended. Brook, Sheila, Heather, and Becky began letting everyone know who made the team and who didn't. As far as LaMonica could see everyone made it until they got to her name.

"LaMonica Powers, out," two of the cheer instructors said simultaneously. LaMonica couldn't even figure out which ones had said it. She was too overcome with emotion.

Immediately, LaMonica's face felt hot. She had to get out of there before she started crying in front of everyone. As LaMonica made her way out of the lunchroom near the door, she could hear Emily Wolfe laughing and mocking her with the other girls. Even the lunch aide was there, mocking LaMonica right along with Emily. They had a special way they liked to say her name, like something was wrong with her.

"We knew La Mon ugly ca wasn't going to make it, didn't we? That girl has zero coordination. She can hardly make it down the hall without tripping," Mrs. White, the lunch aide, said to all the laughing girls.

LaMonica began running down the hall with tears flowing. She was tripping, trying to keep up with her backpack and homework while getting out of that building as fast as she could.

When LaMonica finally made it down the long hall to exit the building, she kicked the doors open and there was Mama.

Mama had already parked her car and was on her way inside the school building.

"Girl, what's wrong with you?"

"Nothin' Mama. I just want to go."

At this point LaMonica was snottin', crying and speaking in a shaky voice.

"No, I need to know why are you crying like that!" Mama said.

Through tears and a shaky voice, LaMonica said, "I didn't make the team Mama."

"Why? Why not?" Mama demanded to know.

"I don't know they just announced I didn't make the team."

"Who else didn't make the team?"

"Just me, I think."

"Oh nawl. Come on in here, LaMonica. I want to talk to these folks."

Mama marched inside the building with LaMonica following her.

"Mama, that's okay. We can just go. Never mind."

"Oh nawl, I'm gonna get to the bottom of this."

Mama already had it in her mind that this situation was quite similar to a parent teacher conference she had attended a few years ago.

At home, LaMonica was always going on and on about her friend Emily Wolfe. She had even brought home friendship pins they had made and exchanged. Emily had been going home excited about her new friend LaMonica as well. In her innocence, never had she thought to even mention her new friend's race.

On conference day when Emily's parents came to school, LaMonica and Emily met up outside on the playground to wait for their parents. Mama came out from the conference early and sat on the bench while LaMonica enjoyed the playground with her best friend.

They were running, skipping and telling each other stories while holding hands like they always did, when Emily's parents came outside. Emily's mother took one look and was absolutely appalled.

"Emily let go of that girl's hand. Get away from her and come over here."

Obviously Emily's mother didn't know who Mama was.

"Why can't your daughter play with mine?" Mama didn't wait for a response from their shocked faces.

"She's just as good as your daughter or any other child at this school."

Emily's parents weren't used to this type of direct confrontation. They both stood there like deer in headlights.

"Come on, LaMonica, let's go!"

Mama was walking fast to the car, and LaMonica knew she had better keep up with her.

Once they got inside the car Mama said, "Them folks is prejudiced. They don't like you because you're mixed and Black. Stay away from that girl."

"But Mama, she's my friend."

"You ain't got no friends. You understand me? The sooner you learn that the better off you'll be."

When Emily and LaMonica returned to school things were a lot different. Her parents had given her a whole lot of philosophies about people like her and Mama. She now hated LaMonica for no other reason than the fact that her parents didn't approve of Blacks, and especially the ones who lived on the east side.

"My daddy works in the plant and we live on the west side of town. My mom said that makes us upper middle-class and you and your mother are low-class.

"My mother also told me you're just a half-breed nigger!"

LaMonica didn't even know what the word half-breed meant, but she knew about that word nigger. Mama had taught her about it because she came from Mississippi and had endured a lot of hardships picking cotton as a sharecropper with Paw Paw. Hearing this word infuriated LaMonica.

Emily Wolfe would torment LaMonica with words like this daily. She would sit next to LaMonica on purpose, get real close to her ear and whisper, "You half-breed nigger!"

One day she couldn't take it anymore. Emily had stirred up so many bad feelings in her that she reacted without thinking. It was in the middle of the week and Emily was all fired up to torment LaMonica per usual.

"My dad makes $40,000 a year working at the plant and my mom says your mother only brings home minimum wage, because you're a low-class nigger and we're upper class."

Before LaMonica knew it she had stabbed Emily with her pencil and the whole classroom was in an uproar. That was the first time she had gotten suspended from school. Things only went downhill from there. Emily Wolfe was popular at school, so it didn't take long for the entire school to turn against her.

Prior to Emily Wolfe tormenting her, LaMonica hadn't been a horrible student. Oh sure, she had always been talk-ative and had attention issues, but nothing like the behavior she displayed from that point forward. Now everyone in the whole school called her names, but it was only when *she* reacted that the school had a problem with any of it. And now instead of best friends, she and Emily Wolfe were arch enemies.

IN MAMA'S MIND, today was no different than when Emily's parents tried to exclude her daughter a few years ago.

LaMonica hadn't made the cheerleading team because she was mixed race. LaMonica wasn't quite so sure. She just knew she was different in every kind of way (including her personality). As a person, she was usually rejected. Now Emily Wolfe and the other kids at school often called her a reject too.

Mama reached the cafeteria. LaMonica was crying harder at this point. Some of her emotions came from the rejection, and some came from the fact she knew Mama was about to escalate this situation.

"Yeah. I wanna know who's in charge of cheerleading here?" Mama demanded.

That's when the two-faced lunch aide, Mrs. White, spoke up.

"Hello Mrs. Powers. These nice young ladies were kind enough to take time out and come teach our young ladies some cheers. But they have to get going. I can help you. What's the problem?"

"I want to know why LaMonica didn't make the team?"

Amid all of this, LaMonica could hear all the other girls high-fiving each other and making plans to meet at each other's houses to practice cheers.

"Okay, ladies. Practice is next Wednesday. Take these forms home for your parents to sign. And let's get ready for the Cougar's big game in two weeks." Brooke said.

"Yay!" Everyone was shouting and cheering.

The girls were leaving the cafeteria chanting,

"We are the Cougars; we can't be beat. Because we've got the power to knock you off your feet. Boom, boom, boom, boom."

THIS BACKGROUND NOISE was echoing in LaMonica's ears and making her feel more and more unwanted.

Then Mrs. White finally answered Mama. "Mrs. Powers, you know how La Mon - ugly I mean LaMonica is. It's hard for her to follow directions and she just can't keep up. Maybe she can participate in some of the other activities we have coming up."

"Don't think I don't see what's going on here."

"I don't know what it is you're thinking, but I've explained it to you as best I can," Mrs. White retorted.

"Come on, LaMonica, let's go!"

In obedience, LaMonica grabbed her stuff and was right on Mama's heels walking out of Kempton. The both of them couldn't get out of there fast enough.

Mama backed out of the driveway like she was mad. You could tell Mama was angry. She began speaking to herself out loud in her "angry voice."

"They don't want nobody Black to take part in nothin' out here. I started to say something more to that woman.

" 'Uh, you know how LaMonica is' What is that supposed to mean?

"Nawl, I know how y'all are.

"LaMonica just do your work and tend to your own business. Don't worry about being on any of these people's groups or teams. They don't want someone like you participating, anyway."

"But Mama Gillette and her sister Gwen play in basketball, and they're Black."

"Yeah, that's because they live over here and they're **all** Black. If you were *all* White or *all* Black, you'd be okay with these folks. But because you're mixed, they won't ever accept you.

"I've told you time and time again, stop running up behind folks! I don't bring you to school to make friends or even to join groups. You are here every day to get your lesson out. Do you understand me?"

"Yes. Okay, Mama."

3

MS. ELEANOR

LaMonica began reflecting on the first time she found out why she was different. She was only a small child, and a White lady showed up at Mama's front door. She looked like an angel. She was tall with long blond hair and was carrying an armful of clothes.

The blond-haired angel entered the living room and all LaMonica could manage was to just stare at her with wonder because you didn't ask adults questions when they were in the middle of talking.

"I brought some clothes for LaMonica," the angel said.

"Oh okay," Mama responded.

LaMonica just continued to stare at the golden-haired angel. No one like this ever came to Mama's house. LaMonica began noting everything about her. Aside from being tall with blond hair that reached her bootie, she had blue eyes, and she wore a beret hat.

For some reason LaMonica felt drawn to this lady, and she didn't want to miss not one single detail about her. Details were especially hard for LaMonica, so this made her continue staring at the visitor intensely to get the job done. This looked quite awkward.

The visitor never spoke to LaMonica directly, she only spoke to Mama about LaMonica.

"I'll be bringing her some more clothes by here soon, Mrs. Powers."

"Okay. That's fine," Mama responded.

"Yeah, I'm gonna be trying to find me a job. And I moved into an apartment down the street on Washington, so I can come visit more often."

Mama didn't say much in response. She had that look on her face that meant she wasn't in agreement with something but didn't feel like arguing.

And just like that, as quick as she had come, the blond-haired angel was gone.

"Who was that, Mama?" LaMonica asked.

"That was your mother."

"But Mama, aren't you my mother?"

"Yes. But that's your real mother, Angie."

"Oh."

LaMonica was dumbfounded. And that's how she found out she was adopted. Mama said Angie used to come by and visit when LaMonica was a toddler, but she couldn't remember.

"Mama, what did I do when Angie came to visit me back then?"

"The same thing you did today. Just sit there and stare at her."

"Oh, okay."

"Look, I'm yo' Mama. But Angie is your real mother."

And that was the sum total of "the adoption talk."

LaMonica focused again on what Mama was saying as they rode in the car.

"Now I've got to hurry up and get us home. I'm meeting with a new tenant today who's probably going to start babysitting you while I work my security job."

"Mama, I'm in the 6th grade. I don't need no babysitter. I can stay home by myself."

"LaMonica, you know you don't like staying home at night by yourself. And my security job is going to be adding me on mostly nights. So we've got to hurry home to meet her.

"And you know I don't like being late. Because you had to stay after school for that cheerleading thang - we're leaving out in traffic when everybody's getting off of work. Now I've got to fight traffic again. Lord have mercy."

"But Mama, can't I just go next door to Ms. Eleanor's house when you work nights?"

"Ms. Eleanor is getting too old to watch you. She's gonna be needing somebody to look after her soon."

"Mama. I don't need a babysitter!" LaMonica said loudly and with authority.

"LaMonica, don't keep going back and forth with me. I've made up my mind, and this is what's best for you. I've already talked with the lady on the phone. She's a friend of the family who just moved here from down south. She needs a place to stay and you're going to need a babysitter when I start working more. So there ain't no need of you going on and on about it. And that's final."

LaMonica's impulses to tell Mama what she thought was best were not easily turned off. But she didn't want to get into trouble, so she thought it would be best to distract herself from Mama by thinking about something else.

For one thing, LaMonica knew that Mama was just doing what she always does and being overprotective. Everyone knew this about Mama, that she was overprotective with LaMonica. A lot of it had to do with the fact that LaMonica had heart surgery when she was younger.

In LaMonica's mind, once she had the surgery, she was healed of the hole in her heart. She felt like Mama acted like everyone was still in the waiting room at the hospital— waiting to see if she's gonna make it. All LaMonica could think of was those soap operas she sometimes watched with Mama and someone exclaiming, "Are we out of the woods yet?" Mama acted like they weren't out of the woods yet.

But honestly, LaMonica always felt the safest when she was near her. In her earliest memory of Mama, she was about two years old and Mama still carried her around like a baby. But even now she was still Mama's baby to protect. And she knew to always act like Mama's baby if she knew what was good for her. Mama had a weird soft and hard side to her. It was definitely a balancing act for LaMonica to stay on the right side of things.

LaMonica brought out Mama's softer side from the time she began babysitting her for Angie. She was a sickly baby that required heart surgery to live. Angie would leave LaMonica for days and even weeks with Mrs. Powers.

Finally, when Angie left LaMonica for a long sprint, Mama stepped up and petitioned the court to become LaMonica's adoptive mother. LaMonica's father Chuck fought against Mrs. Powers but didn't win. The courts gave Angie one year to make things right as a mother or identify Chuck legally as LaMonica's biological father. When the one year court date resumed, Angie was nowhere to be found and Mama became LaMonica's legal parent.

Mama impressed the judge in the courtroom because LaMonica was so well behaved for a one-year-old. He said he knew she was doing a good job with her. Aside from that, Mama was taking great care to get LaMonica the medical help she needed, like the heart surgery she required to live and her follow up care. She often drove LaMonica down to Detroit for special Cardio appointments.

When LaMonica was living with Angie things were very erratic. Because of her illness, she often cried excessively even for a baby and disturbed the partying Angie and LaMonica's father Chuck had going on.

They wouldn't know what to do with her during those times, so they would run her right over to Mrs. Powers - for her to take care of her. That's when Mrs. Powers became aware of LaMonica's illness and decided she would save this child. Through the process, she fell in love with her.

Quite honestly, LaMonica wouldn't even be here today if not for Mrs. Powers. She always required **extra** attention because of her heart condition. And ultimately, that's why Mama watched over her particularly close. And she knew that. So LaMonica decided she would make peace with having this new babysitter.

As they neared the 5th & 6th Street exit sign on the highway Mama declared, "Well LaMonica we're back in Nigga-town".

Mama said this each time they left the suburbs and neared the hood they lived in because you never knew what was awaiting you once you arrived on your street block. It could be something as simple as a drunken wino had passed out and needed an ambulance. Or something as crazy as "Rifle Woman" shooting at her man in the neighborhood. One thing's for sure: there was never a dull moment in the hood.

Mama and LaMonica pulled up to the big, two-story, yellow house on 5th Street. Luckily, the new tenant/babysitter hadn't made it yet. LaMonica saw that the neighbor, Ms. Eleanor, was outside on the porch.

"Mama, can I go over and talk with Ms. Eleanor?"

"Sure, but don't stay too long because I want you to come and meet the new babysitter after I get done talking with her. And you know how you tend to stay at folks' house too long and run anything in the ground LaMonica."

"Okay, Mama. I won't."

LaMonica loved being around Ms. Eleanor even though she was elderly, because she treated her like she was special. Anything LaMonica did, Ms. Eleanor acted like it was the most fascinating, exciting thing she'd ever seen. She was always nice and rarely in a bad mood.

LaMonica started doing some of the cheers from cheer tryouts on the porch for Ms. Eleanor. Amazingly, she was on time with the beat and did a magnificent job (or so she thought).

"Wow. Look at you! You could be a dancer if you wanted to."

"I wanna be a cheerleader."

"Well, that too! You are so good at everything, LaMonica. You can do anything you set your mind to."

"But I didn't get in. I didn't make the cheer team. The other girls got in, but not me.

"I wasn't even doing this good at cheer tryouts."

Ms. Eleanor probably wasn't the best judge of good cheers or keeping in time with the beat, but LaMonica was oblivious to this.

Suddenly the memories from cheer tryouts started flooding her. LaMonica started getting upset at this point. She began reliving the whole cheerleading experience all over again. *Why can't I just have friends and fit in somewhere with somebody?* She thought.

"I bet if Mama would have let me take tap and ballet like

the other girls in school, I would have been ready for cheer tryouts like everybody else.

"I wish I had enough money to pay for my own dance classes."

The more LaMonica talked about her losses, the more bad feelings and memories she drudged up.

Ms. Eleanor just listened.

"Back when I was in the Girl Scouts, I remember when I gave my mission statement everybody laughed at me. I had studied all the Girl Scout books to get ready for the meeting to receive my first pin. I love helping people, so I used the example mission statement for helping others from the book.

"Everybody liked what everyone else said, but when I said my mission was to make the world a better place, everyone laughed, including the Girl Scout leaders."

LaMonica was crying at this point.

"I just want friends."

"Well, maybe the kids at school haven't accepted you, but you'll find like-minded people LaMonica. Don't worry. Your personality is so vibrant one day they will find you." Ms. Eleanor explained.

"How? Even the kids at First Ward don't like me. They tease me and call me Mexican in the after-school and summer program."

LaMonica was crying at this point because she couldn't understand how people in her own neighborhood didn't accept her. It was bad enough she wasn't accepted across the bridge on the west side, but not even in her own hood was she accepted. Not for real.

"Listen honey, you don't need acceptance from any of these groups - First Ward, school, or where ever.

"The only person you truly need acceptance from is

Jesus Christ. And He's already given it to you. You just have to accept Him too.

"Listen, Jesus wants to be your number one best friend. Do you remember that paper I gave you that talked about it?"

"Yes. But I already got baptized at church Ms. Eleanor."

"I'm not talking about going and getting dipped under some water because the folks at church say you're old enough and it's time. What I'm talking about is having a personal relationship with Jesus.

"I'm talking about making Jesus your best friend. Once you do that, you can pray and God will bring the right people into your life at the right time. Some will come for a season. Some will be a blessing. And some will be a lesson. But you'll get stronger about the people who reject you because you know in your heart that by Jesus you are fully accepted. That makes you God's child, and that's all that matters."

LaMonica listened to Ms. Eleanor out of respect for the elderly, but in her mind this was all a bunch of doo doo. *How can Jesus be your best friend?* She thought. *And how does **any** of what Ms. Eleanor just said match the problem she brought up in the first place?* This conversation hadn't gotten her any closer to having friends or being accepted by anyone.

Old people are always talking about Jesus. Thinking about Jesus just made LaMonica think about church. And honestly, she wasn't accepted there either. Oh, they had loved her when she was little and cute without any mouth. But now that she was twelve many of the ushers were always getting on her to be quiet, stop moving around, control herself, stop laughing etc. etc. One usher had even remarked to another - right in front of LaMonica, that they fully expected for her to end up in Juvenile Detention one day.

"Mrs. Powers can't do nothin' with that gal," one whispered to the other.

"Yeah. You know her real mama was a White woman who used to run the streets."

They had their whispers about Mama too, LaMonica just hadn't caught them yet. But she could feel it, how they felt about them. Every week the church put the bulletin out and they listed each family in alphabetical order as to how much money they had put in church. Most of the well-respected families at Mt. Olive worked in the GM Plant. When you scanned past their names in the Sunday weekly bulletin it read $50, $75, even $100 paid into the church. When you made it down to Ella Mae Powers - $5 and LaMonica Powers $1.

Mama was a widow and a single parent raising LaMonica alone. She just didn't have it like that to put into church.

LaMonica began hearing Mama calling her to come home from next door. She was standing in the door singing LaMonica's name - the way she did whenever she was in a good mood.

Almost like Snow White on a Disney movie singing to the dwarfs. You not only heard, but you could feel the notes of happiness coming from her.

"Lah Mon ih caaaaaa time to come home," Mama sweetly sang.

This singing of LaMonica's name could only mean one thing. Mama must have really liked the new tenant/babysitter, and she was moving in.

"Here I come, Mama," LaMonica responded.

"I gotta go, Ms. Eleanor."

"Okay honey and you remember what I said. Jesus wants to be your best friend."

4

THE TENNANT

When LaMonica made it inside, there was a lady who was around Mama's age sitting on the couch. She was brown skinned like Mama, and remarkably they looked like they could be sisters.

"LaMonica, this is Ms. Demona. Demona this is LaMonica."

Ms. Demona stood up and she and LaMonica shook hands all formal like. LaMonica took a seat in the green lounge chair near the couch.

"Well LaMonica, I'm gonna be living upstairs and helping yo' Mama out with you."

A thought came to LaMonica. And for a moment she got excited. Even though Ms. Demona was older like Mama, maybe she had kids her age that would move in too.

"Do you have any kids?" LaMonica asked excitingly.

"No, honey. Sorry I don't have any little blessings to keep you company."

A look of hurt came across Ms. Demona's face. Mama caught it and tried to move LaMonica on to the next subject.

"LaMonica, why don't you go grab Ms. Demona a soda pop out of the fridge to drink."

"Okay, Mama."

When LaMonica came back with an orange soda pop, Ms. Demona was remarking on how nice the area looked. LaMonica could see how someone would think that if the timing was just right.

Mama's yard was always immaculate. She had a white picket fence with flowers donning the walkway to the entrance of the house. Across the sidewalk there was another patch of lawn on Mama's property, and she always edged that up with a knife herself. Down the side of the house near the driveway, Mama had decorated the yard with an iron wheel painted white with flowers planted nearby.

Mama's yard was a refreshing place to look at in the hood. Every time Mrs. Powers pulled up in the driveway, she would immediately pick up any random papers that winos and other foot traffic had casually thrown down on the ground.

Mama was a proud homeowner and very involved in the neighborhood association at First Ward Community Center. Her particular block on 5th Street was between Kirk Street and Norman Street. It didn't have a lot of houses on it because the Mary Bethune Park was across the street and took up a lot of space. Eleven homes in total were on that block. In nine out of eleven homes, the residents were homeowners.

Most of the homeowners were older and took some pride in their home, none to the degree that Mama did, but still they took pride. But most of the other blocks on 5th Street and its surrounding areas were occupied by renters and dope houses. And as you could imagine, papers were everywhere. There was broken glass, even shell casings from shoot outs.

Just around the corner was 4th and Kirk Street with The Sportsman's Bar nearby on 3rd. The intersection of 4th and Kirk Street had a name that everybody in Saginaw knew about. It actually helped Saginaw earn its nickname "Sagnasty" after the city was blighted as one of the most dangerous cities in the US per capita.

Everything around Mrs. Powers was run by a street gang and dope dealers that sold drugs openly on the neighborhood blocks two streets over and every street from 4th and Kirk all the way back to where the numbered streets ended on Washington.

Gunshots could often be heard at night from either drug deals gone bad or the bar located back on Kirk Street. But on that one brief stretch of block on 5th Street between Kirk and Norman where Mama lived, things were pretty cool.

All the people in the neighborhood respected Mama. They'd often see her with her security uniform when she was leaving out to go to her second job. Mama would be strapped up with her gun when getting in the car for work.

She had left LaMonica home alone a couple of times when she worked late night concerts. LaMonica had become scared of the shooting sounds coming from 4th Street because Mama wasn't home.

Once, when Mama was working a late night security shift, she thought she heard someone rattling around near the side door, so she called the police. The sounds of outside seemed to be magnified when she was home alone at night. She no longer had the peace of mind in the middle of dogs barking, people outdoors fighting, and random gunshots going off that she would have when Mama was home.

LaMonica wasn't entirely sure if this was just her being a

scaredy cat or if someone was truly trying to break in. No one had ever broken into Mama's house before, because they respected her. But LaMonica wasn't sure. She knew the kids who lived a few blocks away in the projects near First Ward would never be this scared to be home alone. But then again, they all had sisters and brothers to keep them company.

LaMonica reflected on calling the police that night.

"911, what's your emergency?"

"I think somebody is trying to break into our house and I'm scared."

The 911 operator could tell immediately that LaMonica was not an adult.

"How old are you honey?"

"Ten," LaMonica responded with anxiety.

"Please hurry because I'm scared."

"Okay, just stay on the phone with me and I'll let you know when the officers are there. It won't take long."

The police made it there rather quickly, and they searched around the house and the block. They found Dave "the wino" walking around the block and brought him into LaMonica's view.

"We found this guy walking around, but he says he knows your Mom."

"Oh yeah, that's just Dave. He's always outside at night. No, he wasn't trying to break in."

The police let Dave "the wino" go and came inside to take a statement from LaMonica. When they were about to leave LaMonica didn't want them to go.

"Can you stay here with me until my mom gets home, cuz I'm scared?"

"No, sorry we have to go. We're police officers, not babysitters."

The police incident is probably why Mama is so firm about making me have a babysitter, even though I'm about to be going to junior high soon, LaMonica thought.

"Mrs. Powers, all your neighbors have such pretty flowers planted. You're so blessed to live in such a pleasant neighborhood." Ms. Demona said.

"Oh thank you, honey," Mrs. Powers replied.

LaMonica could not believe that Mama was sitting here acting like this was a wonderful neighborhood. Somebody should warn this lady. LaMonica couldn't control her impulses any longer.

"But Mama, this neighborhood ain't good."

"LaMonica hush."

Mrs. Powers couldn't believe LaMonica had spoken these words right in front of company. She hoped this didn't deter Ms. Demona away from moving in upstairs and being LaMonica's babysitter.

It didn't.

"Can we go look at the upstairs one more time?" Ms. Demona asked.

"Sure," Mama replied.

LaMonica followed them up the stairs. Mama and Ms. Demona were laughing and talking about people in the family and friends they knew from down in Mississippi.

The entire time LaMonica was thinking, *Ms. Demona needs to know the truth about this neighborhood before she moves in.*

There was something about absolute truth that LaMonica seemed to value more than most people. Oh, Mama had high values. That's where LaMonica had gotten her morals from. She and Mama were different from a lot of the people in the neighborhood.

But LaMonica took truth to its limit. She had a hard time not telling it expressly. Like that time when her brother Richard had gotten married, and the preacher called for all of the groom's and bride's families to stand up in the church for a family prayer. LaMonica had taken that seriously. The minister had said 'the Powers family' and Richard's wife's family 'the Armstrongs' were bound spiritually to pray for and help this marriage. When Mama's friend Maxie stood up along with the family, this deeply bothered LaMonica. She took vows with God very seriously.

Even though Maxie was an adult, LaMonica felt it was her duty to correct her. As soon as the wedding party was dismissed into the church's foyer LaMonica made a beeline to go find Maxie and let her know only family was supposed to stand up and make that vow. Other wedding guests heard this, and Maxie was promptly embarrassed. When LaMonica arrived at the reception hall, Maxie came and told her she was out of place for saying that to an adult and she had better not do that again.

LaMonica felt this same urge to expressly tell the truth now. She could barely contain herself. She wanted to interrupt Mama and Ms. Demona so badly and tell Ms. Demona what the neighborhood was actually like. Her face expressed this, and she kept darting her eyes between Mama and Ms. Demona. A couple of times she pursed her lips to talk and Mama caught her. Mama shot LaMonica a look, and she knew what that meant. So she breathed in deeply through her nose and gritted her teeth together hard to avoid speaking.

She then decided it would be best for her to go back downstairs and let Mama and Ms. Demona talk. The impulse to blurt out all the information she had about the neighborhood was just too strong.

LaMonica went and made herself a snack in the kitchen. She sat down at the table and began thinking about Ms. Demona moving in.

Maybe Mama was planning on having Ms. Demona come with us on our outings and be away from the hood on most days.

Yeah, maybe that's it, LaMonica thought.

Mama tried to keep them active in events far away from the north-east side. They were always at people's homes way out in the country, or at least over at Uncle Charlie's house in Sheridan Park.

The north-east side, or as Mama liked to call it, "Nigga-town" was quite possibly the worst part of Saginaw. Most times Mama figured out a way to get her and LaMonica out of "Nigga-town" for the day. They attended events like airplane shows where they were pretty much the only Black people there.

Mama was also a member of a club called Parents Without Partners or (PWP). PWP met frequently and some-times older couples with children made love connections or single parents would just enjoy each other's company while the children in the group had playdates and made arts and crafts.

PWP events are how LaMonica and Mama spent most of their holidays. Most of the members had big, beautiful homes. Some were out in the country and some were in the suburbs. The homes in the country had horses for LaMonica to brush and learn about. Obviously the atmosphere was in complete opposite of the hood they lived in, but LaMonica still honestly enjoyed it.

Everyone was nice to her and Mama, and she never felt like they were the odd people at PWP (like she did at the airshows). Even though they were normally the only Black people at these meetings and events as well. No one at these events seemed to question LaMonica's blackness, which was very opposite to the treatment she received at the gatherings she attended with Mama that were predominately Black.

Every time Mama and LaMonica crossed the 5th and 6th Street exit to return home Mama would declare again, "Well LaMonica, we're back in Nigga-town. Let's see what these niggas been up to today."

That meant Mama knew she had to go home and pick up stray papers and trash thrown in their yard from winos and people's children who had parents that didn't know how to watch them properly.

It also meant there may be some hood entertainment for them to watch. Like fights, people getting arrested and running from the police, somebody passing out from drugs and alcohol. You just never knew with the north-east side.

In the early 1980s, before renters took over the area and before crack fully hit the small city of Saginaw, crimes in the hood were almost comical. There were mostly just winos walking around in the neighborhood.

LaMonica and Mama would sit on the steps on warm nights and the winos would pause while walking and say, "hello."

Dave "the wino" was a regular.

"Can I get a little spare change? I don't mean no harm, ma'am. I don't mean no harm."

Sometimes LaMonica's cousin Joy would spend the night and sit on the stairs with them. The winos would sometimes stop and offer each of the girls a quarter instead of asking for change like usual.

"Hello Mrs. Powers. Can I give the girl's a quarter? I don't mean no harm. I don't mean no harm."

On warm days, especially in the summer time, a wino would often pass out from drinking and being out in the sun too long. LaMonica would be anxious when the ambulance showed up.

Mama would calm her fears by saying, "Oh, he'll be alright. They just need to take him on up to Bay City to get dried out." That meant he needed to go to the rehab and get help to get off alcohol. This rarely worked, though. Actually never, never had LaMonica seen it work long term.

Living on the north side could be entertaining, though. Mama and LaMonica would often watch crimes right from the porch. The arrests and police chases were great. They didn't even really need TV.

One time they watched the police chase a car up and down 5th and 6th Streets. These are both one-way streets and after a while the suspect was going the wrong way up 5th. He just kept circling the block though, and eventually the police caught him.

LaMonica and Mama were on the steps. Mama was cheering for the police.

"Yeah, get that fool. Ahh yeah, they got 'em now LaMonica. He's going to jail now."

Mama owned a police scanner, so she already knew he had held up a store at the mall and that's why he was running from the police. She was always on the side of the police. LaMonica could tell she secretly wanted to be a police officer herself, but had settled in life for being a security guard.

Growing up, LaMonica was taught that the police were her friends, but they will beat your ass if you get out of line. She often accompanied Mama to meetings with the Police Community Relations Commission (PCRC) which Mama was a board member of.

Maybe Mama was telling Ms. Demona that this was a good neighborhood because that's truly the way she felt. Nothing scared Mama. When people would shoot in the neighborhood and LaMonica would get scared, Mama would tell her - "You scared for what? I got something to bust back at these niggas if they get too rowdy."

Mama was the original pistol carrying Madea, way before Tyler Perry ever came out. Gun shots in the ghetto didn't bother her a bit. But she did know when it was time to instruct LaMonica to get down low when the shooting came too close to the house.

But more than anything Mama found what would be scary to people from the suburbs, downright entertaining. Like "Rifle Woman" whenever she got upset. "Rifle Woman" was a lady who lived in the neighborhood that was quick to shoot. Mama nicknamed her that. Anytime "Rifle Woman" got into it with her boyfriend or other females in the area, she would pull out her rifle and start shooting at them. Thank God she was a bad shot, because as far as LaMonica could remember no bullets had ever landed on a person. LaMonica and Mama would be in the windows and back-yard trying to get a view of who "Rifle Woman" was shooting at.

Mama would declare, " 'Rifle Woman' is at it again," and she and LaMonica would both laugh.

As far as LaMonica could guess when Mama grew tired of "the entertainment" she branched outside of the north-east side neighborhood. Not all neighborhoods she and LaMonica visited were White. Sometimes they went over to Uncle Charlie's house and LaMonica would play jump rope and have fun with her cousin Joy.

Uncle Charlie was very pro Black, but he never made LaMonica feel out of place. Or like she wasn't Black enough to be a part of the family or the Black community. He treated her like family, REAL FAMILY.

Uncle Charlie was better off than Mama was. He lived in Sheridan Park. A predominately middle classed Black area in Saginaw. This Black neighborhood was nothing like the hood Mama and LaMonica lived in. The houses were newer and nicer. Most people worked in the GM Plant and had good salaries. Crime was relatively low. Uncle Charlie was always trying to convince Mama to move from over there on 5th and Kirk.

A thought crossed LaMonica's mind.

That must be the kind of neighborhood Ms. Demona thinks this is. What with all the nice lawns and pretty flowers on Mama's block. She thinks this is a nice middle classed Black neighborhood. Well, looks can be deceiving if you stop by during daylight. And if she moves in, she will soon find out, LaMonica thought.

LaMonica heard Ms. Demona and Mama coming down the stairs.

"So when can I move in?" Ms. Demona asked Mama.

"Well, things are ready for you now, so as soon as you want to."

"Alright. I'll be here this evening with my things," Ms. Demona said.

"Okay then. We'll be here waiting on you," Mama said.

Ms. Demona headed out the door with a promise to be back soon to move into the upstairs apartment.

Ms. Demona ain't from Sagnasty. When night time rolls around she ain't gonna know what hit her, LaMonica thought to herself.

Oh well. I tried.

5

THE BABYSITTER

Ms. Demona moved in that night. She had some men in pickup trucks carrying her furniture up the stairs, and Mama was helping to direct them. LaMonica decided she would rather stay out of everybody's way in case somebody asked her to help with something, so she went in her room to read a good book she had been holding onto from the library.

When they finished Mama came in LaMonica's room and told her Ms. Demona was all moved in. She said she'd be going in to work early in the morning and Ms. Demona would see her off to school. That way they could get to know one another.

"When you wake up in the morning, I'll already be off to work. I'm leaving before 5 a.m. to see my first client, but Demona will be here to help get you situated."

"Okay, Mama. Goodnight," LaMonica responded.

Now that Ms. Demona would be living with them, this would free Mama up to make more money. She could take extra Home Health Care patients at 5 a.m. and do her security jobs in the evening without worrying about how

LaMonica would get breakfast or dinner or get to and from school.

LaMonica woke up the next morning around 6:30 a.m. She smelled bacon in the air, just like when Mama was home making breakfast. The first thing she thought about that morning was the letter Randall from South Junior High had written her. She had hidden it under the mattress so Mama wouldn't find it. He had placed his cologne on it, and LaMonica didn't want Mama to end up smelling it when she came into the room. She also didn't want to get rid of it because she enjoyed reading his words over and over again.

Randall was Gillette and Gwen Hampton's older brother. He was in the 7th grade and would often come up to Kempton to walk them home from school. Sometimes LaMonica would be outside waiting on Mama past 3:30 when she was running behind and still working with a patient. Gillette and Gwen were always staying after school for sports or band practice.

On those days Randall and LaMonica would stand out in front of the school together. He would often remark on LaMonica's long hair and imply that she's pretty. They started talking about South School and which are the easiest teachers there. LaMonica would be going to South Junior High next year.

"What's your favorite subject?" Randall asked.

"None of them," LaMonica replied.

"Come on now. I know you've got to be good at English with all those books you carry around reading."

They both laughed. Because it was true. LaMonica always had a ton of books in her book bag from the school library. She absolutely loved reading. But she was super clumsy. Her backpack was often too heavy, pulling on her little short frame and causing her to drop books.

One day she had so many books in there she could hardly zip the backpack up. The backpack fell from LaMonica's back and all the books came toppling out. Randall had helped her pick them up and sort them in a neater way, so that the book bag would zip up.

"Just sit that bag down over there against the post until your Mom gets here. That way it won't keep falling. Trust me LaMonica nobody is gonna steal a backpack full of books."

They both laughed. She had followed Randall's suggestion every day since.

LaMonica was very careful to stay on the lookout for when Mama would pull up, so she could not seem like she had been talking to Randall. Mama didn't play when it came to boys. She really, really didn't play. She told LaMonica under no circumstances was she to ever be talking to boys until she was old enough to be courtin'. And that wouldn't be until she was way up in high school and nearly grown.

Mama might threaten to whip LaMonica for a lot of things and never go through with it. But for boys, she knew Mama would pull out her leather security belt strap and whip her tail good for even talking to a boy.

LaMonica had begun to look forward to Mama running behind with a patient. It gave her and Randall an opportunity to talk which she otherwise wouldn't have had. The last time they had had that opportunity was three days ago. He had handed her a folded up note and told her not to read it until she got home.

LaMonica could smell his cologne on it right away as soon as he passed it to her. She couldn't wait for Mama to go to bed that night so she could sneak and read it.

She had to sneak to read it because Mama was always keeping up with her.

If she was in the bathroom too long - "LaMonica what's taking you so long, you alright in there?"

If she was upstairs washing clothes too long - "LaMonica I've done been heard that washer start. Why are you still up there? What are you doing?"

And she had very limited privacy in her bedroom due to the fact that the door had been removed years ago. Anyone walking by could see in full view whatever was going on in there.

Mama was a super light sleeper, so turning a light on in the house was out of the question. The times she had tried it- "LaMonica what are you doing with that light on in the middle of the night?"

Mama even expected her to walk to the bathroom at night with no lights on.

So LaMonica had taken the note and waited until Mama fell asleep and very quietly without making her bed creak she opened the curtain and read it by moonlight.

"*DEAR LAMONICA. You have to know by now I have a crush on you. More than a crush, I have feelings for you. You are so beautiful inside and out. I know you can't even see it. And to me, that makes you even more beautiful.*

I think about our talks after school long after they happen. You're on my mind at dinner time, when I'm doing my homework and even when I fall asleep at night. I wish we could go to the movies together or even just talk on the phone sometimes. But I know your mom is strict. And she would never allow that.

When you come to South, I want you to be my girlfriend and we can spend a lot more time together there.

You have my heart girl. Please say yes.

. . .

WITH LOVE,
    Randall"

LAMONICA HAD BEEN DEVISING different places to hide the
note ever since she had brought it home. Mama may have
been a security guard, but she had the qualities of a detective. She had found several things that LaMonica had tried
to hide before, including her diary.

It would only be a matter of time before Mama found it
under the bed, so LaMonica decided to go ahead and read it
again since Mama wasn't home and then put it in her jean
pocket.

Just as she was placing the letter in her Jordache jeans
she looked up and saw Ms. Demona standing in her
doorway.

"What is that you just put in yo' pocket, LaMonica?"

"Nothing."

"Well, it didn't look like nothin' to me. Looked like a
folded up note."

LaMonica was a horrible liar. She couldn't come up with
anything, so she just stood there dumbfounded.

"Girl, hand me that letter that is in yo' pocket **now**!"

LaMonica handed the letter over to Ms. Demona with
embarrassment.

Ms. Demona smelled it deeply first. Then she spoke.

"Um, nice cologne," she said mockingly.

Then she began reading the letter. LaMonica felt so
embarrassed. The more she thought about the words that
were on that paper, the more embarrassed she felt.
LaMonica would look on the floor and then look up again at
Ms. Demona. It seemed like it was taking forever for her to
finish reading such a brief letter. And her face wasn't giving

any indication of what was going on in her mind. She hadn't spoken a word since she'd remarked on the cologne.

Finally, Ms. Demona finished the letter after what felt like an eternity. She slowly pulled the page away from covering her face and her eyes appeared. She glared at LaMonica with what could only be described as hate.

"Who the hell does yo' fast tail think you are having a boy write you a letter like that?

"You sitting up there meeting with a boy at school and letting somebody get that close to you.

"Have you let him play under your clothes yet?"

"What?" LaMonica exclaimed in disbelief.

"Girl, don't you say what to me.

"I've been watching how you talk to yo' Mama. Answering her with yes and no. You're supposed to say yes ma'am and no ma'am when addressing adults.

"And don't you ever in yo' life say what to me!

"Yo' mama gave me full permission to whip you if I need to. And I will grab a switch and tear yo' tail up if need be.

"Yesterday when I was moving in you didn't even come and help. Ain't no way any of my nieces or nephews from down south would have been so rude. Or maybe you just don't know a doggone thang since ya mama babyfies you so much.

"All I know is if you think this boy likes you for anything more than playing under your clothes then you ain't got the sense God gave a fool."

"Uh huh, he does like me. We talk about books and all kinds of things. We don't even talk about nasty stuff.

"And I am smart. I won the spelling bee for the entire district last year. And my mama says I'm smart."

"Girl, have you lost yo' got dang mind? Ooh, if you were my child, I would slap the mess out of you right now.

"Mrs. Powers ain't taught you not to answer adults back?

"I would get a switch and whip you right now. But you've got me so upset if I hit you I might break yo' narrow tail in two.

"LaMonica you ain't nothin' but a fool right. Mrs. Powers' family was right about you. You ain't gone turn out to be nothin' but a lil' whore like yo' mama.

"Because ain't no way a boy wrote you a letter like this unless you was actin' fast with him first.

"Now I want you to show me that boy when I drop you off to school, so I can tell him a thang or two."

"He doesn't go to my school Ms. Demona," LaMonica said.

"Then how are you meeting up with him?"

"He comes up there after school to wait for his sisters."

Demona should have understood some of this from the letter, but she had become so angry with LaMonica that she could hardly think straight.

"Okay, well, I want you to point him out to me when I pick you up after school today. And it seems like you and that boy may have either been gearing up to have sex or are having sex. So If you don't want me to tell yo' mama that's what's been going on, you'd better keep everything that happened today between us."

LaMonica was only twelve years old and still a virgin. But if Ms. Demona told Mama something like that, she would most likely believe her. LaMonica was routinely in trouble, and it would be her word over the word of an adult. She decided she had no choice but to listen to Ms. Demona.

LaMonica went to school that day and when Ms. Demona came to pick her up she was hoping she had forgotten about the incident. It was just her luck that Randall was up at the school early. She saw Randall before he saw her and waited on the other side of the school building so she wouldn't have to talk to him or get caught near him when Ms. Demona pulled up.

As soon as Ms. Demona pulled into the school's front driveway LaMonica jumped in the car and Ms. Demona demanded to know if that was Randall standing in front of the building.

LaMonica hesitated.

"Answer me gal or I'm gonna have to tell yo' mama you've been having sex with a boy."

LaMonica wanted to defend herself against this lie. She hadn't even thought about sex. But after what had happened between her and Ms. Demona this morning, she knew better than to defend herself.

"Yes, that's him."

"Excuse me, what did you say? Yes what?"

"Yes ma'am," LaMonica said out of compliance.

"That's what I thought."

Ms. Demona preceded to get out of the car. LaMonica rolled the window down just a crack so it wasn't noticeable, but she could still listen.

"Hey young man, is your name Randall?"

"Yes ma'am."

"Well, I'm Ms. Demona. I'm helping Mrs. Powers out with LaMonica."

"Oh yes. I'm friends with LaMonica."

"Yes. That's what I'm here to talk to you about. I found your little letter and LaMonica doesn't need any friends at this time. Especially not any friends that are boys. I'm working with Mrs. Powers to help get LaMonica under control. She comes from a rough background."

"A rough background?" Randall asked.

"Yes. She actually was one of those drug babies."

"Listen, you seem like a nice young man. I can tell by the way you carry yourself. What's your last name, Randall?"

"Hampton," Randall quickly responded.

"Hmm Hampton, Hampton. I'm new in town but seems like I've heard folks mentioning attending the church of a Reverend Hampton. Any relation?"

"Yes. That's my grandfather."

"Oh wow. You come from a good family, too. Randall, you don't want to get involved with a girl like LaMonica and hurt your family's reputation. I'm sure your family has plans for you to attend college and have a good life."

"Yes ma'am. I'm going to take over the church after college."

"Well, you continue making us proud in the Black community, Randall. Don't get caught up with girls like LaMonica and I won't have to report this back to your grandfather."

"Yes ma'am. But what about LaMonica? I don't want her to get into trouble. It wasn't her fault I gave her that note."

"Well, I'll tell you what Randall, LaMonica will not be waiting after school anymore because I'll be here to pick her up on time. But once she reaches South Junior High, I need you to promise me you won't have anything to do with her. And as long as you do that, I'll make sure Mrs. Powers isn't bothered with this incident.

"Can you do that, Randall?"

"Yes ma'am. I can do that as long as LaMonica will be Okay."

"Oh, don't you worry about LaMonica, Randall. She's gonna be just fine."

Demona walked away going towards the car and muttered underneath her breath, "She'll be just fine after I whip her no count narrow behind into shape."

6

THE PURSUIT OF FREEDOM

Well, obviously having a boyfriend is out of the question, LaMonica thought. She had awakened early Saturday morning ready to undertake the morning cleanup routine with Mama as usual.

Almost every Saturday Mama and LaMonica dusted, vacuumed, mopped, washed windows and gave the two story home with two add on apartments upstairs, a complete, thorough cleaning.

However, on the Saturdays when Mama saw a good rummage sale in the newspaper, they would skip cleaning that Saturday and have fun garage sailing for the day. LaMonica enjoyed this much more than cleaning.

Mama didn't believe in people doing any sort of physical work on Sundays, because she said, "That's the Lord's day." So Mama would make up for Saturday's deep cleaning during a couple of her lunch breaks from work, while LaMonica was in school. This suited LaMonica just fine, because she didn't enjoy cleaning anyway unless it was with a group of people, like back when she used to help her friend Gloria Contreras clean house with her family.

Gloria's mother required an even deeper clean than Mama. They would not only dust, vacuum, mop, and wash windows, but they washed walls as well. Mrs. Contreras didn't play. She said if any of her six kids' friends wanted to come to her house on a Saturday, they would have to partake in the family clean up party.

LaMonica had met Gloria one day at the park across the street. She had just moved into the neighborhood. On some stroke of luck Mama had allowed LaMonica to go to the park that time, (while she sat right there near her on the bench, of course).

When Gloria entered the park she and LaMonica somehow gravitated towards each other. Everyone thought they were twins. It was remarkable how much they looked alike. Even Mama saw it.

Gloria had begun coming over to play at LaMonica's house almost every day after that. Even though she was only about ten years old, she was responsible for babysitting her infant brother. Mama would take care of the baby so Gloria could just be a kid and have fun with LaMonica.

Mrs. Powers didn't trust too many people with LaMonica, but she had gotten to know the Contreras through LaMonica and Gloria's friendship and had finally felt it was safe enough for LaMonica to visit without her.

Gloria's family took LaMonica on as another sibling. She had four brothers and an older sister, and they protected LaMonica like she was one of their own. LaMonica felt so free when she was with them.

Mama had even allowed her to start going places in the neighborhood on her bike with them. Prior to that, Mama had only allowed LaMonica to ride her bike on the sidewalk directly in front of the house on 5th Street. But not too far towards Kirk Street and not too far towards Norman Street.

Generally LaMonica could be seen boringly riding her bike from the big yellow house to just before the end of Kirk Street (which is three houses away). Then she would turn her bike around and ride three houses past her big yellow house towards Norman Street.

LaMonica was the only bike riding age child in the neighborhood stuck doing this. Everyone else at least could ride the sidewalks around their entire block. So when Mama started letting LaMonica ride all over the neighborhood with her Mexican friends, she was happily surprised. She didn't ask any questions until one day she tried to do that alone.

"Mama, can I go ride my bike around the corner to the store?"

"Girl nawl, that's too dangerous."

"But Mama, you let me ride to the store with Gloria and them all the time," LaMonica whined.

"That's because you have Gloria and all her brothers to protect you. You're a girl and an only child, LaMonica. It's not safe for you to be riding your bike around the neighborhood by yourself. Somebody might try to pick you up and put you in their car," Mama warned.

Richard and Deb were adults by the time Mama adopted LaMonica, and so she often referred to her as an only child.

When Mama remarked someone might try to kidnap LaMonica that scared her. *Ahh, so that was it! That's why Mama lets me go all over the place with Gloria and them because I'm well protected.* This spoke to the anxiety inside of LaMonica, so it made perfect sense to her.

Yes, Mama was right. The guys in Gloria's family certainly protected her. One time LaMonica had ridden her bike to the St. Joseph's Thrift Store (St. Joe's) while Gloria and her sister walked alongside her.

Gloria's brothers weren't far behind. While LaMonica, Gloria and her older sister Selena shopped inside, the boys were walking up. Someone from outside came in and told them, "Hey your brothers are out there fighting somebody."

They all ran outside. Some random dude had grabbed LaMonica's bike while she was inside of St. Joe's Thrift Store shopping and had made their way down the street on her bike. Abel, one of Gloria's brothers, ran down there and caught up with him.

Everyone was watching the whole incident from the front of the thrift store. Abel started beating the boy off the bike, then he brought LaMonica's bike back to her, like it was nothing. Just another part of his day. LaMonica was so wowed! She had told Mama the exciting news as soon as she made it home.

The Contreras had picked up and left Saginaw when Gloria's father received a job offer, making a lot more money in Florida. Oh, how hard that day had been for LaMonica. The day her beautiful "twin" had packed up with her family and left the state. They said they would write and keep in touch, but they never did.

That was nearly two years ago. And now LaMonica was stuck back at square one, no friends and riding her bike back and forth in front of the big yellow house on 5th Street.

❧

When LaMonica had gotten up and dressed that Saturday Mama had cooked a big breakfast like she always does. Eggs, bacon, toast, applesauce and Malt-O-Meal were all on the menu. She had gone into the hallway and yelled up the stairs for Ms. Demona to join them.

"Good morning," Mama said in her singing voice.

"Would you like to come have some breakfast with us?"

"Oh yes," Ms. Demona responded as she came quickly down the stairs.

"I was upstairs smellin' all this good food down here. I was hoping' fo' an invitation."

"Awe honey, you don't have to wait for no invitation. We've got plenty of food around here. You're welcomed to it," Mama said.

"Good morning, LaMonica," Ms. Demona said.

"Good morning, Ms. Demona."

LaMonica had noticed that Ms. Demona was quite a bit nicer to her in front of Mama.

Mama was looking through the classifieds at all the rummage sales going on.

"They've got some good rummages going on today. Some are way out there in the township too."

"What's a rummage?" Ms. Demona asked.

"You've never been to a rummage sale?" Mama asked Ms. Demona.

"I don't think so. What is it?"

"It's where folks sell stuff from their house real cheap, usually on the weekends. The further outside the city you go, the better stuff they have."

"Oh, okay yeah we say, 'garage sales' where I'm from."

"Garage sales, rummage sales. Same thing," Mama explained.

"Chile, I bet they sell some nice stuff at garage sales here up north."

"Oh honey, they do. That's where I got all my curtains

and bedspreads from. Some of my furniture too. If I'm lucky, I can catch an estate sale and clean up."

"I got most of my clothes from there too," LaMonica chimed in.

"You did! Girl nawl, not all them beautiful clothes I've been seeing you wearin'. I thought yo' mama had spent a fortune," Ms. Demona exclaimed.

"Well, some of her clothes I get from JC Penney, cuz I have a card with them. But for the most part me and LaMonica hit these rummage sales, and she grabs up all kinds of stuff for less than $5. That's why she's got more clothes than she knows what to do with now."

"I'll tell you what let's put these dishes up for later and go hit these sales," Mama suggested.

LaMonica thought quickly. If Mama had Ms. Demona to keep her company, maybe she could stay home by herself for a change and just chill. Even though she enjoyed garage sailing with Mama, she would enjoy some time to herself even more.

"Mama, can I stay home and watch MTV? I can do the Saturday cleaning while y'all are gone and you wouldn't have to make up for it on your lunch hours this week."

"Yeah, Ella Mae, why don't you let her stay home and be a pre-teen for a little while. We won't be gone for too long." Ms. Demona admired how much quality time Mrs. Powers puts in with her child, but frankly it was too much. She had made that child her best friend. Demona wanted to talk about adult grown women's conversation without LaMonica around. And besides, she had to deal with LaMonica herself every day and she needed a break from being around her.

"Okay. You can stay home. But don't you open the door for nobody. And I'm gonna call and check on you."

"Alright Mama."

LaMonica was so happy when she saw Mama and Ms. Demona back out of the driveway. Now what was she gonna do first? Because she would definitely save the cleaning up part to the last possible moment.

LaMonica decided she would put on some of Mama's expensive clothes. Mama had a beautiful black sequenced jazz singer style dress LaMonica loved to dress up in. She also had furs and fake diamond clip-ons LaMonica often liked to get into when Mama wasn't home.

Mama had all sorts of makeup in the bathroom. She liked to blend dark brown foundation with light foundation in order to get the perfect makeup color for her skin. So LaMonica was able to make her face up with the light toned makeup before getting dressed.

She decided this would be a model shoot. After doing her make up LaMonica did her hair, put on her mother's special clothes and stood in front of the big mirror in the bathroom, making camera clicking sounds and acting as if she was a model in New York.

She soon grew tired of that though and watched a movie based on Los Angeles Mexican gangs. Their fashion and Spanish accents got her pumped up. LaMonica stopped watching the movie and raced around the house for something similar to throw on. She put chola dark burgundy lipstick on and wore a bandana with a baseball hat. Then she began speaking in a deep Spanish accent in the mirror.

"Mi familia came to this country the hard way. Oh da lay. And we'll kill you to get what we want. You don't want to mess with La Raza."

LaMonica admired herself in the mirror. She looked like a true Mexican. Most of the people in the hood assumed she was at least part Mexican, anyway. She could unquestionably pull off being a Mexican actress.

The phone rang. *Oh snap, that's probably Mama.* LaMonica had been so caught up in her fantasy world that she hadn't even begun to clean anything. She raced to grab the phone.

"Hello."

"Hey LaMonica."

It was Mama.

"Girl, we found some good sales today. You almost missed out, but I grabbed you a few things. We're getting ready to grab us something to eat from 7-Eleven. You want a polish sausage and a Slurpie?"

"Yes."

"Okay. What kind of Slurpie do you want?"

"Um, cherry cola, if they have it. Thank you, Mama."

LaMonica's mind began racing. Ahh shoot, she hadn't done any cleaning yet and needed to race like crazy to get it done before Mama made it home.

She thought to herself. *Okay, there's no way I can get everything done in time. So what's the most noticeable things in the house?*

Dusting. She decided.

LaMonica grabbed the Pledge wood furniture cleaner and a dusting rag and made a mad dash to clean all the wood downstairs quickly. Then she decided she should probably hurry and vacuum.

After vacuuming, LaMonica took a bit of Pine-Sol and put it on any dirt spots on the floor in the bathroom and the kitchen. That way she could just wet those spots and not have to wait for the whole floor to dry.

Everything looked and smelled pretty good. Hopefully Mama wouldn't notice she hadn't done the windows or anything upstairs. LaMonica honestly didn't mean for it to happen like this, but time just got away from her.

Mama and Ms. Demona made it home, and they both were excited about their garage sale finds.

"Ooh, it smells good in here, LaMonica," Mama said.

"Sure does. Like Pine-Sol," Ms. Demona added.

Then they both sat on the couch showing LaMonica their finds from garage sailing.

LaMonica breathed a sigh of relief. She had passed the cleaning inspection.

7

LAMONICA WITH "THE GOOD HAIR"

I n the second half of the school year, Ms. Demona decided she needed to make some money from working. She wanted to honor her commitment to help Mrs. Powers with LaMonica for free room and board, but she definitely needed a way to have some actual cash in her pocket.

Together she and Mrs. Powers came up with a plan. Demona could get in as a housekeeper on the evening shift where Mrs. Powers worked. She would still be able to pick LaMonica up from school. Then she could drop LaMonica off at First Ward Community Center's after-school program and head to work.

Mama would be off from her first job in time to pick LaMonica up from First Ward and take her home. Then Mama would get ready for her security job. LaMonica would only have to stay home by herself a couple of hours at night when Mama worked security as opposed to all night, like before.

LaMonica only kind of liked this plan. Not having to be home with Ms. Demona when it was study time was definitely going to be a plus. Even though Ms. Demona had not spoken to her as harshly as she did with "the Randall letter" she was still harsh when it was time to do homework.

LaMonica dilly dallied around a lot, especially if she had any math homework. It was particularly hard for her to sit in one spot for a long length of time and complete math homework. She was always bouncing around and putting her mind on something else. When Ms. Demona would catch her doing this, her patience would run thin. She would speak to LaMonica in a slow, dark and deep hateful tone.

"Get. Yo' ass. Ova here. And sit down gal!" Ms. Demona would yell.

LaMonica enjoyed doing homework in groups. She had a good time at First Ward in the summer because there were parents from all over the city who brought their kids there for "the Black experience."

Black parents who worked in the GM Plant or had high levels of education lived in the suburbs, or at least good neighborhoods. In order to make sure their kids had some exposure to their own roots, they would send them to First Ward Community Center's summer program. Where the children would learn African drum, dance, take soul food cooking classes and more.

First Ward was centered dead in the projects. In the summertime, there was a mix of project kids and suburb kids. But parents didn't bring their kids across the river to First Ward after dark. So there would only be project kids in the after-school program in the fall and winter.

The project kids could be very blunt with LaMonica.

"If you're Black, then why is your hair like that?"

"Why you don't look like yo' mama?"

"Is that yo' **real** mama or yo' grandmama?"

Even the after-school workers who weren't familiar with LaMonica's mother would ask her to speak Spanish. One after-school leader would often ask her to help teach him Spanish.

"I don't know how y'all speak that fast talkin' language. I tried to take a year of Spanish and I couldn't learn it."

LaMonica would just agree and grin with anyone who assumed she was Mexican, which was pretty much everyone at First Ward. Because of her long, silky texture hair and her skin tone, they would not accept her as Black. And White people were absolutely hated in the projects. So LaMonica didn't argue when they called her Mexican.

THE SECOND HALF of 6th grade proved to be more and more interesting. The Saginaw Public school district made an astonishing ruling that year. They decided that Handley Elementary would become a gifted school. Half of the school was already set up for accelerated learning. But the Board of Education decided only students who were gifted would remain at the school from that point forward.

All students who weren't in the gifted program were given the option to take the gifted test. If a student didn't pass or their parents refused the test, then they were reassigned to the closest elementary schools.

As a result, Kempton became quite full with new students in the second half of the year. One of those students was a young girl named Lisa McDonald. Lisa was mixed raced, Black and White. LaMonica finally found herself in the company of someone else who looked like her at school.

Lisa and LaMonica became fast friends. They exchanged

phone numbers and called each other every evening and on the weekends. As the weeks passed by, after seeing how excited the girls were about each other, Lisa's mom Beth made a phone call to Mrs. Powers.

"We've got to get these girls together, Mrs. Powers. I'm tired of hearing them begging to spend the night every weekend."

"I can bring LaMonica by this weekend and we can all get to know each other," Mama replied.

Mama and LaMonica went over to Beth and Lisa's house on a Saturday. It turned out Lisa lived on the east side near Uncle Charlie and she was a part of open enrollment for out of district students like LaMonica.

Beth was White and Lisa's father (who wasn't in her life) was Black. They lived in a lower middle class neighborhood. Even though it was on the east side, it wasn't nearly as violent as where LaMonica lived on 5th and Kirk.

Lisa had a brother and a sister who looked like her. After meeting them, LaMonica wondered to herself what it was like to grow up with brothers and sisters who looked like you.

Mama and Beth got to know each other while LaMonica and Lisa enjoyed their visit together. Mama determined that Beth seemed stable, and it looked safe enough for her to allow LaMonica to come over and visit at Beth's house with Lisa. So the girls began having sleep overs and pajama parties at each other's houses.

Beth was a little nervous about the neighborhood that LaMonica and Mrs. Powers lived in, so she tried to encourage the visits to be at her house as often as possible.

The more LaMonica started coming over to Lisa's house, the more she got to see what everyday life was like in Lisa's neighborhood. And in Lisa's neighborhood, she was "the princess." Lisa was definitely into boys. And she loved how all the boys swooned over her and fought for her attention.

Once LaMonica started showing up, the guys in the neighborhood began giving her attention too. They remarked on how long LaMonica's hair was and how pretty she was. Lisa did not like this. After walking to the store one day with LaMonica and hearing the boys go on and on about how fine LaMonica was, she had had enough.

Lisa switched up and said she was sick. Beth called Mrs. Powers to come and pick LaMonica up early for the weekend. And Lisa started socializing more with the kids that came from Handley and becoming distant with LaMonica at school.

LaMonica felt like her hair was the problem. People were always remarking on how beautiful and different her hair was. It was the key thing that made her appear "to not be Black" at First Ward. It was the main reason the boys in Lisa's neighborhood liked her, and now Lisa was distant with her.

She decided she would cut off all of her long, beautiful hair. LaMonica had asked Mama several times if she could cut her hair or even simply just have some bangs. But Mama had refused every time. Mama knew how impulsive LaMonica could be sometimes, so she even went through the motions of hiding all the scissors in the house.

One Saturday when Mama and Ms. Demona were out rummage sailing, LaMonica took the butcher knife and chopped off most of her hair in the back and gave herself some bangs. When Mama returned, she was horrified. Surprisingly, all Ms. Demona did was laugh.

"Well ain't no since in whippin' her Ella Mae. It's done now."

Mama took LaMonica to the hair salon at JC Penney so

they could try to straighten out her botched haircut. They did the best they could with what they were working with.

When LaMonica returned to school Monday Lisa began talking to her again like nothing had happened. Secretly she couldn't wait for all the boys in her neighborhood to see LaMonica's hair now and say that *she* was the prettiest girl in the neighborhood once again.

Mama had noticed the difference in LaMonica and Lisa because they weren't calling each other or visiting each other anymore. She had asked LaMonica about this several times.

"LaMonica, why don't you and Lisa talk anymore? What's going on?"

"Nothin' Mama. It's nothing going on."

When Lisa and LaMonica suddenly became fast friends again, this perplexed Mrs. Powers. She decided she would watch the situation before allowing them to visit with each other again.

8

A TIME TO EXPLODE

O ne Friday, Mama invited Ms. Demona to come to the bingo while she worked there as a security guard. This meant LaMonica would have to come too, since bingo was at night and no one would be home to sit with her.

LaMonica enjoyed bingo because they had a kitchen where they made tacos and the people who operated it had two daughters that she liked to talk to. All the members from The Old Tymer's group (the senior outreach division of First Ward) were there every week to run the bingo.

It was Mama's job as the security guard to keep order in the bingo and to follow the winner of the Jackpot out to their car for protection. She also escorted the board members to the bank for the money drop off.

Mama was also a member of the Old Tymer's group, and the other members had known LaMonica since she was a toddler. They were always glad to see how nicely she was growing and would give her a lot of attention when she was there.

It wasn't uncommon for members to buy LaMonica

snacks or run out to the car and excitedly give her crafts they had made. Someone was always walking up, patting her on the head and giving her well wishes and love. She was a favorite of theirs.

Ms. Demona observed all of this.

The only horrible thing about the bingo was the cigarette smoke. It choked LaMonica and burned her eyes. She didn't know how Mama could stand it each and every weekend, which is why, despite the good people there, she only went every blue moon.

The next morning, on the way to school, Ms. Demona seemed to be in an uptight mood.

"So I guess you smellin' yo' self since you going to junior high school soon, huh?"

LaMonica didn't know how to respond to that. If she responded the wrong way, it could be taken as disrespect. If she didn't respond at all, it could be taken as disrespect as well.

"You got all them people at the bingo gushing over you. But not everybody was gushing over you. Your own family wasn't."

"My own family?" LaMonica finally responded.

"Yep. Yo' mama told me that "the Lincoln's" from yo' daddy's side of the family were there last night. And guess what? They didn't say anything to you. She said every time you've ever come to the bingo they were there and didn't even say a word to you. Because they don't care nothin' about you."

LaMonica just had a sad, lost look on her face. She was stunned and didn't know how to respond.

"Yeah. So now that summer is near and you about to go to junior high, I hope you ain't gone give yo' poor mama no problems. Her family already can't understand why she adopted you. What with your daddy's side of the family being drunks and yo' real mama being a whore."

LaMonica did everything in her power not to speak. But she looked at Ms. Demona with pure hatred. Her lips had involuntarily turned up in Elvis Presley like fashion.

"Gal you betta fix yo' face! Mrs. Powers told me how the last time yo' real mama was in town she was running up and down 5th Street with some other prostitutes hustlin'. Don't get mad at me cuz yo' mama's a whore. Just do better."

When they made it to school, LaMonica jumped out of the car feeling so angry, but she had no one to direct it at. She wasn't allowed to address Ms. Demona without physical discipline from her and later Mama. So she started thinking of all the nasty things Emily Wolfe had said to her over the years in school. LaMonica decided that she couldn't wait for Emily to say some of her hateful, "I'm better cuz I live on the west side, because I'm White and you're not" mess. She was gonna straight up slap her dead in her face today!

And that's just what she did. The first time Emily even began with the slightest of an insult LaMonica hauled off and slapped her across the face. By early morning they suspended her.

Mama had to leave work to pick LaMonica up because the principal wanted to talk with Mama directly. She couldn't send Ms. Demona.

"Mrs. Powers, LaMonica has to learn to control her emotions and her temper. Even if the other student said mean words to her, she can't act out in anger and get physical.

"Because it's so close to the end of the school year, I really should suspend your daughter for the rest of the year. But I know how hard you have been working with her and her behavior. Even to the point of hiring on extra help, so I will let her return after three days. But Mrs. Powers LaMonica will need to write a letter of apology and we will not allow her to engage in the end-of-year summer games."

"Okay, thank you, Mr. Padilla," Mama replied.

"Come on here, LaMonica," Mama was ticked off. She had to leave work for this mess.

Mama began fussing at LaMonica as they walked to the car.

"Why can't you keep yo' hands to yourself?"

"But Emily is always whispering to me and calling me a half-breed nigger, Mama."

"Well, why don't you tell the teacher?"

"The teacher never believes me."

"I'm dropping you off at home with Ms. Demona. I have to get back to work. I just don't have time for this LaMonica," Mama said.

Mama dropped LaMonica off and backed out of the driveway, headed back to work to finish her shift.

Demona felt satisfied that everything she had spoken about LaMonica had come true. She spoke to her in a slow, deep, hateful tone.

"Look at you, LaMonica. You ain't no good. You ain't no earthly good."

"Now ya done got ya self suspended from school."

"I told yo' mama you wasn't gonna turn out to be nothin' but some ole trash cuz you came from trash. Looks like I was right."

"Yo' poor Mama after everything she's done for you too. You are so ungrateful."

LaMonica tried to take herself away from the situation mentally. She started imagining what it would be like to be with her father's side of the family. She knew they loved her because he had come around trying to see her on multiple occasions, but Mama wasn't having it. Maybe she could find him.

LaMonica was so deep in thought she had tuned everything around her out. The TV, Ms. Demona, everything. The next thing she knew, she felt a switch going across her butt and back.

"Girl, you must have lost yo' got dang mind, sitting up here ignoring me while I'm talkin' to you."

"Ahhhhhhhh. Please stop. Stop. Stop. Please!" LaMonica wailed and wailed while Ms. Demona gave her lashes with the green limb also known as a switch from outside.

"Yo' mama told me I had permission to beat yo' tail if you got disrespectful, especially after you got suspended today."

"You ain't gone get suspended from school and then lie around here day dreamin' all day."

"Oh nawl you gone be cleanin' up this house and makin' up all yo' school work."

"Now get yo' ass in your room and start on your schoolwork, before I break you in two."

9

LITTLE MS. MEXICANA

Sixth grade ended and somehow miraculously LaMonica passed to the seventh grade. She was headed to South Junior High in the fall.

LaMonica was excited for the summer that year. One day when she was sitting on the stairs, she saw an unfamiliar girl across the street at the park. This new girl had long silky hair. She appeared to be Mexican, and she was getting the attention of all the boys in the neighborhood.

LaMonica's immediate reaction was jealousy. She had a scowl on her face and her lip turned up involuntarily, like Elvis while looking at her. Somehow the new girl didn't pick up on her body language and came across the street from the park and introduced herself.

"Hi my name is Luciana but everybody calls me Luchie. Me and my family just moved down the street what's your name?"

"My name is LaMonica."

"We just moved in the neighborhood, LaMonica. Do you want to come to the park with me?"

Luchie spoke with a beautiful Latina accent. When she

said LaMonica's name it sounded like La moan ee kah. She was warm and friendly, and LaMonica found it hard not to like her.

Mama was still just as guarded when it came to LaMonica's safety as she had ever been. But somehow when it came to Latinas, she almost felt more open to LaMonica interacting with them. That's who accepted her as a friend and family. And Mama could see it too. LaMonica didn't necessarily fit in with the people in the ghetto, and she definitely didn't fit in with the people at school. But somehow she fit in with Latinas.

Now of course Mama would not release the reigns yet and just let LaMonica run around the neighborhood with Luchie like she did with Gloria a few years ago. But she was open to letting her go across the street to the park without her.

Mama observed Luchie's demeanor and thought, *This young girl seems nice.*

Luchie began coming over every single day to visit with LaMonica on the porch and to sit on the stairs. Sometimes they would go to the park while Luchie was babysitting her little brother or nieces and push them in the swings. Their personalities clicked, and they just had fun together.

They began to tell each other secrets. LaMonica divulged that she was adopted, but with one little white lie. She told Luchie she was mixed - half Mexican and half Black. It was a good thing the blond-haired angel only *called* now. She had stopped coming around for years, so no one would know the truth.

LaMonica was excited to be close to someone again. She felt happiness once more. She had become so disheartened between Mama's overprotection and Ms. Demona's meanness that she wanted to get away from the big yellow house on 5th Street. There seemed to only be darkness all around her until Luchie came in her life and became a light. She now could see her way clear to freedom again. Just like when she was friends with Gloria and the Contreras.

Mama eventually met Luchie's mom and her siblings. Luchie was the second to the youngest of her siblings. And all of her brothers and sisters, except for her little brother Emiliano, were adults. They all had pleasant, vibrant personalities like Luchie. Mama felt like she could trust them, and so she began to let LaMonica go down to Luchie's house and spend time with her and her family.

LaMonica loved it there. Luchie had nieces and nephews that she could play games with. Being raised as an only child at Mama's was lonely. She had often wished for siblings. Helping Luchie babysit seemed like fun to her.

Eventually Mama started letting LaMonica have sleep-overs at Luchie's home that summer. LaMonica began spending all day and most nights at Luchie's household with her family that summer. She loved hearing the stories of how they used to live in Mexico and what it was like back then.

Luchie's baby brother Emiliano was half Black and half Mexican. They accepted LaMonica as being like him and they took her in as family. Not only that, but they felt the need to help her learn her "own culture." They saw Mrs. Powers as a pillar of the community and a woman of integrity. But in their mind's she had missed out on introducing LaMonica to her heritage. "Her Mexican heritage." They endeavored to help give it to her.

LaMonica immersed herself in the Mexican culture. She went to Quinceañeras, (Sweet Fifteen Celebrations) and Mexican dances. Anywhere there was a Mexican party, she was there. Mama let her go too, just like with the Contreras.

If she was going with Luchie's family Mama felt she was safe.

Now, honestly, Ms. Demona was happy to have her summer free, so she did not put up any kind of opinions or fuss about LaMonica being gone so much. Ms. Demona had found herself a boyfriend. And that's where she was when she wasn't at her evening job. She was happy spending most of her time with him.

Mama was busy working. She took solace in the fact that LaMonica was safe having fun with her Mexican friends, and she really didn't give it a second thought.

Luchie and her family continued to add the Mexican culture to LaMonica's life. They taught her all sorts of new Spanish phrases and words. Only Juana (Luchie's mother) spoke fluent Spanish, but everyone in the house spoke Spanglish (a mixed of Spanish phrases and English). They all had Mexican accents when they spoke, and LaMonica developed one too.

If her Spanish sounded too plain they would say, "Girl, you sound like a pocha (bad Spanish speaker of Mexican heritage). Roll your Rs like a Mexican rrrrrrrrrrr!"

It was almost like an episode in the movie The Color Purple when Nettie was walking around the house teaching Celie how to read and write with tags on all the items. It was a similar experience when Luchie and her family introduced LaMonica into the Mexican culture.

LaMonica would also share things from the Black culture. She introduced them to Black movies and books about African Americans. A lot of the facts on African American inventions that Uncle Charlie had taught her she passed on to them. And Mama would sometimes send down soul food to the house, and they absolutely loved it.

LaMonica and Luchie were both thirteen at this point.

Traditionally girls plan their Quinceañeras (Sweet Fifteen Celebrations) at this age. LaMonica and Luchie would often plan their dresses and colors for their Quinceañeras. They talked about who was going to be "standing up with them" (their escorts). LaMonica found out a Quinceañera was almost just as expensive as a wedding. She knew full well that Mama would never pay for something so extravagant. But she planned it with Luchie all the same.

10

THE THREE AMIGOS

With LaMonica so immersed in the Mexican culture and being a nicely developed thirteen-year-old, this caused the Mexican boys to take notice of her. She was now a part of the Mexican community.

Usually when she went to dances, she did the cumbia (a Mexican group dance where everyone dances in a circle). One evening while at a dance, Luchie's cousin Juan came over and asked her to dance. They danced to a beautiful slow Mexican love song. She knew it was a love song because of the beat and the fact that the words *mi corazon* (my heart) were used a lot. LaMonica and Juan had a love connection right away.

Juan and his family had recently moved near Luchie and LaMonica around the corner on 6th Street. Juan began coming over to Luchie's home every day to spend time with LaMonica. LaMonica, Luchie, and Juan were like three best friends. They did everything together. They walked to the neighborhood store, rode bikes together, cooked together and ate together. Everything.

The new three amigos did not escape the attention of Mama. She began coming down to Luchie's house to find out who all was there after she started seeing Juan with the two girls too frequently. Mama had noticed that Juan was always at Luchie's house when she went down to check on LaMonica. She did not like the idea of LaMonica being around any boys.

Mama would've lost it had she known that LaMonica and Juan had become boyfriend and girlfriend. It went even deeper than that. Juan and LaMonica were falling in love. She had finally kissed a boy. Really kissed a boy. LaMonica was still a virgin, but at thirteen her love affair with Juan was getting very intense. They were kissing, necking, and giving each other hickeys. All they wanted was to be with each other constantly.

Juan and LaMonica even had their own song, I Need Love by LL Cool J. Sometimes LaMonica would say that she was at Luchie's house, but then she would sneak over to be with Juan at his house. She would help him babysit his nieces and nephews, and sometimes they would watch movies together. But always, always they would find moments to be alone together and hold one another. They would stare deep into each other's eyes; say I love you and kiss.

Mama had caught Juan with LaMonica at Luchie's house one too many times. She began to feel like this could not be a coincidence. So she asked LaMonica about it.

"How come every time you're at Luchie's house I see that little boy down there? Who is he?"

"Mama, that's just Luchie's cousin Juan."

"Well, I don't like it. Girls don't have no business being alone with no boys."

"Mama, we're not alone. We're always in groups. It's

always me, Luchie, Luchie's sisters and brothers, and Juan."

What LaMonica was saying was only half true. Yes, Luchie had a large family and whenever Juan was over they were all present, but somehow, they found Juan and LaMonica's relationship to be cute. They allowed them to be alone upstairs in the home, provided they left the door open. This didn't stop them from kissing all over each other though, because the family rarely went upstairs to check what was actually going on.

Now Mama's love of the police force and her security work made her an excellent detective and researcher. She wasn't buying it. Mama made it her mission to check up on LaMonica constantly now. She still let her visit with Luchie as she was watching the situation.

Mrs. Powers began showing up unannounced at the places she knew LaMonica would be with Luchie. A new family, the Delacruz's, had moved into the neighborhood around the corner from Luchie and LaMonica. They were close friends with Luchie's mother and Juan's mother. The Delacruz's had a nice open yard, and they often invited family and friends over to listen to Mexican music and play Mexican bingo.

Mama went to Luchie's house to check on LaMonica one day during the summer, and one of the family members who had stayed behind from the Mexican bingo party told her that LaMonica was around the corner and how to find the house. When she got there she saw LaMonica, Luchie, and Juan all outside together, laughing and joking. This angered Mama she had had enough of pulling up at places and seeing Juan present wherever LaMonica was.

Mama had a way of calling LaMonica's name where you knew she was in trouble. And everyone around knew LaMonica was in trouble that day.

"LaMonica come get in this car now!"

Juan and Luchie looked at each other worriedly. They knew how strict Mrs. Powers was. And they knew LaMonica had received great privileges, being able to be as free as she had been this summer. They could also see that was in danger.

When LaMonica got into the car Mama was angry. Her tone was angry.

"LaMonica, I have told you time and time again to stay away from that boy."

"How come every time I come and see what you're doing, you're with that boy?"

LaMonica knew in this case, this was one of those questions that was really not to be answered. So she just looked at Mama.

"This is my final warning to you. If I spot you around that little boy one more time you will not be allowed to go down to Luchie's house. Do you understand me?"

"Yes, Mama, I understand. Please don't stop me from being friends with Luchie."

"I won't but only if you follow what I said. If I catch you again with that Juan boy I will not allow you to visit with Luchie or her family."

LaMonica and Luchie discussed it. They would have to be extra extra careful about LaMonica and Juan being around each other. Luchie told LaMonica that Juan said he would do anything for her. Including running away together.

"Juan loves you, LaMonica. He says if you guys can't be together he's willing to run away with you. I have some family in Chicago we can go there all three of us and start a new life."

There was no way LaMonica and Juan were going to

stop seeing each other like Mama said. They were too deep in love.

One day when LaMonica was visiting with Luchie, Juan snuck over through the back door. He had climbed the fence from off of 6th Street in case Mrs. Powers was looking down the street.

"I'm babysitting my nieces and nephews. My mom's going to bingo and I want you to come over to the house with me, LaMonica."

LaMonica agreed. She was always happy to be able to spend time with Juan. They jumped the back fence onto 6th Street and hurried up and snuck over to his house.

When LaMonica arrived Juan's mother and family were happy to see her. They gave her hugs as they were leaving for bingo. They all loved LaMonica and they would often smile lovingly at them when they were together.

Most of the family left except for Juan's younger brother Chuey and his nieces and nephews. Juan and LaMonica were in charge of taking care of the little ones in the house. They put some cartoons on for the kids and began slow dancing in the room to their favorite song; I Need Love by LL Cool J. They were staring into each other's eyes and singing the words to each other. It was so beautiful. The love connection was super strong.

Not much time had passed by when Juan's younger brother Chuey yelled up the stairs, "Mrs. Powers is here."

He had already let her in the house.

"LaMonica get down here right now!"

LaMonica came running down the stairs. Juan was in agony over the thought that she was going to get a whipping.

All you could hear as LaMonica and Mrs. Powers were walking to the car was Mrs. Powers cussing LaMonica out.

"What in the world were you thinking having your ass up the stairs with a boy?"

LaMonica began answering. But Mama looked at her and said, "Why are you answering? Have some respect when I'm talking to you."

Mama whipped the car around the corner back to 5th Street and the big yellow house. She screeched into the driveway. Both of them rocked back-and-forth when she finally stopped.

"You are not going back to Luchie's house! You will not be around that boy ever again. It's obvious I can't trust you. I can't trust yo' fast tail!

"I can't believe you. I have told you time and time again about this LaMonica!"

Ms. Demona had already left to visit family for the last two weeks in the summer, when the schools announced the teachers were on strike. Until the teachers, the union and the board of education could reach a financial contract agreement, the school start date was unknown. Mama informed Ms. Demona of this and she decided to remain out of town until the schools opened back up and Mama would need her assistance with LaMonica.

That's when LaMonica, Luchie and Juan made their big plan to runaway to Chicago.

When Luchie and Juan saw that Ms. Demona was gone, they waited until Mrs. Powers pulled out of the driveway for work and snuck down to LaMonica's house to discuss it.

"We'll get all our clothes and keep them in a bag under our beds and then tomorrow night around midnight, me and Juan will come to your window."

"We'll walk as far as we can out of the city and we'll have to hitchhike the rest of the way to Chicago," Luchie explained as she laid out the plan.

Everyone agreed.

When they left LaMonica began packing up her clothes for the next night and put them under her bed like Luchie suggested.

She debated in her mind if she could truly leave Mama and move to Chicago. Her brother and sister Deb and Richard were both adults and lived down south. Deb moved and never spoke to Mama again. Richard called, but he was busy with his own life in Atlanta. Mama often stated to LaMonica that she was the only family that Mrs. Powers had.

This made LaMonica feel guilty somehow. *Was it true what Ms. Demona had said so often? That I'm ungrateful for everything Mama has done for me?*

That thought quickly snapped LaMonica's mind onto Ms. Demona in greater detail. *Mama will tell Ms. Demona everything I've been up to over the summer (if she hasn't already). Ms. Demona will be extra hard on me this school year because of it.*

LaMonica couldn't even take the thought of that. She decided right then and there, yes, she would do it. She would run away with Luchie and Juan to Chicago tomorrow night.

She made sure to be awake at midnight, because she didn't want Luchie to have to knock on the window (with Mama being such a light sleeper).

Luchie and Juan were there on time. LaMonica lifted the window and threw out her bag of clothes. Then she climbed out of the window. Thankfully, Mama didn't hear any of this.

They quietly crept past the house and begin walking in the direction that they thought Chicago was in. They ended up at the Quad Movie Theater in the Saginaw Township, around 1:30 a.m. It was almost September, and in Michigan during this time the nights were getting cold. The three amigos decided to get inside somewhere where it was warm.

Luckily, Meijer's (a 24 hour shopping store) was right next door to the movie theater. So they headed over there. They used the restroom and walked around and warmed up for a bit. Out of nowhere, the store security grabbed all three of them and took them to the back.

"What are you guys doing out here so late at night?" The security officer was smug.

They all gave fake names, but security wasn't buying it.

"LaMonica Powers, Luchie Marin and Juan Rodriguez," the officer offered.

"How do you know that?" LaMonica asked.

"Because there's a missing person's report out about all of you. We've notified the police and your parents are on their way."

Luchie and Juan's family came to pick them up, and Mrs. Powers picked up LaMonica.

LaMonica was quiet on the ride home.

"That's it, LaMonica! You won't be seeing Luchie or Juan anymore! Not only can you not go down there to visit, but she's not allowed at my house either."

LaMonica didn't even respond. She just felt hopeless.

The school strike ended, and LaMonica began school at South Junior High. She wanted to be excited about finally making it to junior high school, but she couldn't because she could no longer see Luchie or Juan or any of her Mexican friends that they all associated with anymore.

Ms. Demona had sent word that she would return to Michigan shortly, but she wasn't back in time to transport LaMonica back-and-forth to school. This worked out well for LaMonica. She was able to convince Mama to let her get a bus pass with the other kids who lived on the east side and went to school near the suburbs.

LaMonica's heart ached for Juan and there was a pit in her stomach from missing her friends. This was her chance to see them again.

Mama had no time to watch what LaMonica was up to in the mornings. She had to get to work. So early one morning when LaMonica was supposed to go to the bus stop, she purposely missed the bus and waited until she saw Luchie on her way to school. They were so happy to see each other they hugged.

"Let's go get Juan!" Luchie said.

They both walked around to 6th Street and caught Juan as he was walking to school. They devised a plan to hide in the woods near the neighborhood school.

They spent all day there, laughing and talking. Poor Luchie had to witness LaMonica and Juan kissing every five minutes in between conversation. But they had intensely missed each other.

Unbeknownst to them, all of their schools had notified their parents that they didn't show up for school that day. And Mrs. Powers, the Marin family, and the Rodriguez family were actively looking for all three of them.

As it drew closer to lunchtime, the three amigos became hungry. They pooled their lunch money together and decided to go get something to eat from the nearby corner store. That's when they were caught.

As it turns out it wasn't noon. The three amigos had no real way of keeping time. It was well passed 4 p.m. and Luchie and Juan's whole family were spread out in the neighborhood looking for them.

Juan's little brother Chuey saw them first.

"There they are!"

He pointed everyone out. Luchie and Juan took off running. LaMonica wasn't able to keep up. Because of her heart condition, she often became winded easily and couldn't run fast.

Chuey caught her and she bit him hard on his chest. Luchie and Juan came back at that point. Luchie and Juan's family put the three amigos in their cars and took them all to Luchie's house.

Mrs. Powers wasn't home, she was at South Junior High talking with the principal trying to figure out what had happened to LaMonica. Luchie's mother, Mrs. Marin, left Mrs. Powers a message on her answering machine that they had LaMonica there with them.

Then Mrs. Marin called Juan's mother, and she came from around the corner. She was not happy that LaMonica had bitten Juan's younger brother. But she was even more upset that Juan would skip school like that.

Mrs. Rodriguez pulled out a belt with metal spikes on it and began beating Juan with it. This was heart wrenching for LaMonica to witness. She knew her friend Luchie would get a whipping with a belt too. And once Mama finally made it there, she would try to whip her as well. But LaMonica had had enough of being talked to like she was dirty and being whipped with belts and switches. She decided she wasn't buying it.

When Mama made it home and heard the message on her answering machine, she was angry and relieved at the same time. Angry that LaMonica would do this and have her so worried and relieved that nothing terrible had happened to her.

When LaMonica saw Mama at the door, she knew it was on. She could tell that Mama's blood pressure was up. Her eyes looked like they were popping out of her head and her cheeks were shaking.

"What happened today?" Mama asked any member of Luchie's household that would answer.

Her adult sister Amalia stepped up.

"Well, apparently Mrs. Powers, LaMonica came and got Luchie to skip school and then they both pulled Juan into it," Amalia explained.

"Yes, and your daughter bit my son Chuey," Juan's mother added.

"Now, we disciplined *our* kids the last time when they all ran away, but we hear LaMonica didn't get a belt to her butt. As a matter of fact, she got brand new school clothes and a new pair of Jordans," Amalia continued.

"We're doing what we need to do to get *our* kids in line, Mrs. Powers."

Amalia could have said more about how Mrs. Powers was spoiling LaMonica, but out of respect for her age she didn't.

Mrs. Powers tried to get LaMonica to apologize for biting Chuey, but she wouldn't. She had taken on some strange, rebellious, angry attitude.

"Well listen, I apologize for LaMonica biting your son, Mrs. Rodriguez. And y'all don't have to worry about LaMonica causing any more problems with your kids because she won't be coming around here anymore. I've told LaMonica time and time again she isn't old enough to be courtin' and she shouldn't be around Juan.

"If she comes knocking on the door to either of your houses, don't let her in. Call me and I'll come get her straight. If I'm not home Demona will be there checking the messages and she'll come get LaMonica straight for sure.

"Let's go, LaMonica."

LaMonica didn't move.

"I said let's go, girl!" Mama screamed with anger.

LaMonica reluctantly followed Mrs. Powers out to the car.

As soon as they got inside Mama started in on her.

"What in the world were you thinking doing all of this?" Mama asked loudly.

LaMonica sat there with her arms folded as Mama drove down the one way and looped back around the corner to get home.

"You hear me talking to you, LaMonica? I said what were you thinking skipping school and running up behind that little Juan boy?"

"What do you expect when you won't let me be around my friends anymore?" LaMonica screamed back with an attitude.

"Look girl from now on, you ain't got no friends. Do you understand me?

"You go to school, you get yo' lesson. You come home; you do your homework. That's it."

"So when can I see Juan and Luchie again?"

"You ain't never seeing that little boy again. Or Luchie either, for that matter. If you go down there they better not let you in or I'm gonna handle them? Do you understand that, Ms. Powers?!"

Mama said Ms. Powers snarky. She liked to use that name with LaMonica when she was making a point that she wasn't in charge. There was only one Powers who had the real power.

11

HE AIN'T "CRAZY" IN LOVE

LaMonica was devastated. Every day when she came home from school, she would barely eat. Mama would have to force LaMonica to eat anything off her plate and then she would go lay in her bed for hours until it was time to change into bed clothes and get up for school again the next day.

The whole atmosphere was different. LaMonica could tell she couldn't sneak down to Luchie's house anymore. They would really not let her in and report her to Mama. She had even seen Juan walking to Luchie's house. He had purposely walked down a side street so he wouldn't have to cross in front of her house. He didn't even want a glimpse of her anymore.

Something had definitely changed. LaMonica didn't know what it was until Mama cracked a joke about it one day.

"That little boy Juan came over here one day while you were in the back room moping around with your head-phones on. I guess he was declaring his undying love for you, hahaha!

"Whoo hoo," Mama continued laughing.

"Yeah, he had some gold chain with him, talking about 'please Mrs. Powers let me give LaMonica this present, I saved up for. I love her.'"

"What Juan came by?" LaMonica exclaimed with excitement and pain at the same time.

"Yep, and I went in there and grabbed my pistol too. I let 'em know not to come around here no more. I told him if he ever, ever, darkens my door step again I was gonna put a bullet in his ass. Now I bet you he went on about his business then. He ain't crazy."

That was it then. Mama had scared Juan. He wasn't coming back, and he was most likely done with LaMonica. She sunk into an even deeper depression then. She began listening to songs in her headphones that wished for death.

She started making statements about suicide and threatening to fling herself from the top of the stairs.

"I hate my life. You're a jailer and this is misery. I should just jump down the stairs and kill myself," LaMonica screamed one day at her mother.

LaMonica shouldn't have expected any sort of empathy, because Black people in her hood laughed at suicide. They didn't take it seriously. The general opinion in the hood was that everybody's too busy trying to survive, to kill themselves. Suicide was an unfathomable term to them.

"Well, I'll tell you one thang if you jump down the stairs, I ain't taking you to no doctor, because I ain't got time for your bull today, LaMonica."

"I'll slit my wrist!" LaMonica declared.

"Girl please. And if you get any blood on my carpet, you will be cleaning it up."

LaMonica decided it was hopeless. She didn't really

want to die. She just wanted to see her friends again, and it was obvious Mama wasn't going to budge.

Even though Mama laughed at the situation with Juan, she hated seeing LaMonica like this. She didn't know how to identify it, but she knew something was wrong. So Mama set LaMonica up with a counseling appointment.

The counselor recognized that LaMonica was depressed immediately. After just one session, LaMonica shared a lot with the counselor because she was warm and believed that children should have rights.

She explained to the counselor how she had always been rejected by Blacks and Whites. And how she had found a community of family with Luchie's people and her Mexican friends. After searching for that for so long and finally to find it, only to have it snatched away by Mama - LaMonica felt like life was hopeless.

The counselor understood. So when Mama pressed her for a quick fix to the problem. She told her the truth.

"Mrs. Powers, LaMonica is changing and growing. She's going through a number of hormone changes. Teenagers face a lot. And in LaMonica's case, knowing that she's adopted and not feeling accepted by her family, neighborhood or school community has greatly affected her.

"Having this community of people meant everything to her. I understand you don't want her dating at such a young age, but aren't you willing to compromise and at least let her have some friends? To tell someone LaMonica's age that she's not allowed to have friends is devastating to them. Teens her age live to be accepted in social groups. She's been accepted by *this* social group. You've essentially removed her will to live."

"Well, I didn't know all of that," Mama replied.

"I'll let her visit with her friends. But I still don't want her around that Juan boy. Ever!"

"Okay. Well, I'm glad you were willing to compromise for LaMonica's sake, Mrs. Powers."

Directly after the meeting, Mama drove to Luchie's house. LaMonica came with her, wondering what in the entire world was going on. Mama informed Luchie's mother and her sister Amalia that she wanted the girls to be able to visit with each other and be friends once again. Amalia and Mrs. Marin agreed. Luchie popped out from behind the door and said she'd give LaMonica a call later.

After that Mama drove to two more of LaMonica's Mexican friends' houses, that she often hung out with with Luchie and Juan. Evidently Mama had told their parents not to let LaMonica associate with their children either, because she feared they would all get into trouble again. Each of the families thought the whole thing of Mrs. Powers knocking on the door and resending her threats were weird, but they agreed to let their children be friends again. Honestly, none of the other parents could imagine being as overprotective as Mrs. Powers was with her child.

Luchie called LaMonica that evening after dinner.

"Hey girl, you know your mom scared the hell out of Juan and his family. It's gonna be hard because I'm so close to the both of you, but Juan definitely doesn't want to be here at the house at the same time that you are. I love both of you guys and I'm sorry you guys broke up."

LaMonica wasn't even sure she and Juan were broken up until Luchie said that. *Wow, I guess he had no way to tell me;* she thought.

Him purposely walking a different path to avoid her house was a big clue, though.

"From now on I'll just come to your house most of the time, girl," Luchie said.

"And if you want to come down here, just call first so I can let you know if Juan's here or not. That way y'all don't ever have to cross paths. Because that's the way he wants it, LaMonica."

"Okay," was the only response LaMonica could muster up. Now she knew it was truly over between her and Juan.

Just then there was a beep on the phone line and LaMonica clicked over. *Ugh,* it was Ms. Demona.

"Well hello there, how are you?" Ms. Demona asked in her mockingly friendly voice.

"Good, how about you Ms. Demona?" LaMonica feigned respect.

"I'm doing wonderful, honey. But don't worry, I'll be back soon."

LaMonica rolled her eyes and clicked back over to Luchie.

"I'll call you tomorrow, Ms. Demona's on the phone for Mama."

Mama always turned the phone up real loud when she was on it. LaMonica could hear Ms. Demona through the phone.

"Hey Ella Mae, what you been up to since I been gone?"

"Chile, been trying to get little Ms. Powers in order."

"Who LaMonica?"

"Yes honey."

"What she been doin'?"

"Chile, she's been actin' a fool! A fool right!"

LaMonica didn't want to hear anymore. She put her headphones on and went and laid in her bed while listening to sad music as usual.

12

SCHOOL DAZE

L aMonica knew Mama hadn't had time to completely fill Ms. Demona in on all of her escapades since she'd been gone. But once Ms. Demona was back, Mama was going to fully inform her on what had been happening. And she could only imagine how much more hateful things would get.

For some reason, Ms. Demona felt like Mama didn't get the recognition she deserved and that taking care of LaMonica was a burden Mrs. Powers had chosen in life. She along with *some* other members of Mrs. Powers' family felt it was their duty to take up for Mrs. Powers against LaMonica. No one felt this more strongly than Ms. Demona.

Anxiety began setting in just thinking about when Ms. Demona would return. If LaMonica felt like she didn't have any freedom now imagine how it was going to be when she came back.

Plus, she was finding it too hard to forgive Mama for making her lose her first love, Juan. And now the relationship with Luchie and her family was strained.

LaMonica's father had come by the house recently again.

This time he had his girlfriend in the car along with a young girl about her age. They stopped in front of the house asking Mrs. Powers if he could come and pick her up sometimes. Instead of saying no like she normally does, Mrs. Powers said, "I'll have to think about that."

This excited LaMonica. Maybe if she went over to her dad's house, she could move in with him. Maybe things could be better. She wouldn't have to constantly hear about the sins of her mother and how she's never gonna be anything over there. She wouldn't have to feel like she was in a jail cell every day.

LaMonica wasn't sure how all of this was going to work out. The only thing she was sure about was that every time her dad came by and tried to see her he always said, "I just want you to know I love my daughter Mrs. Powers. I love LaMonica."

Love being directed at LaMonica as a word was not something she was used to hearing outside of Luchie and Juan. It's not something that Mama said very often, and it's not something that she heard from her adoptive family.

Ms. Demona finally returned. She had to get a new job after staying away for so long, and this new job demanded more of her attention than before. Thank God. So it forced Mama to let LaMonica continue to catch the bus to school, which LaMonica was very appreciative for because she felt like at least she had that little amount of freedom.

See, even though Mama said LaMonica could resume friendships with Luchie and her other friends, things just weren't the same. They felt strained and didn't visit each other much anymore. Once again LaMonica felt like she was locked in a jail cell.

Fitting in at South Junior High started off rocky. LaMonica was bussed in from the east side so she didn't have any connection with the girls who lived in South's school zone. And she certainly hadn't made friends with the ones who came over from Kempton.

She and Monica had long stopped being close, most likely a warning from her mother to stay away from troubled kids like her. And Lisa had chosen to attend North Junior High School instead of South, because it had more Black kids.

The other Black kids that were bussed into South from the east side all had gone to the same neighborhood elementary schools and had a relationship with each other already. And the Mexicans at South were not the same ones that LaMonica went to Quinceañeras and Mexican dances with. She was not one of them. As a matter of fact, one of them had even called her a nigger. Monica had entered junior high with a hair relaxer, looking 100% Latina, and she seemed to be taking up with that segment of the population.

LaMonica was accepted by one Mexican friend, however, Ruby. Ruby was an outcast because of her weight. She was a loner. For some reason the older LaMonica got, she felt drawn to the discounted and counted out people of the world. And so immediately she liked Ruby. They gravitated towards each other and spent every lunch hour together.

During orientation, the school administrators had said that 7th grade would be a period of adjustment for new junior high students. They hit the nail right on the head, especially in LaMonica's case. She was already disorganized and found it hard to keep up with one class in elementary. Now she had several classes to get to on time, keep homework organized and abide by the varying rules each teacher set. LaMonica found this extremely overwhelming.

She did not understand how to verbalize this. It just

appeared to Mama and everyone else that she just couldn't get it together. LaMonica became very disruptive in class. She began operating as the class clown. Almost every day LaMonica was sent down to the Assistant Principal, Mr. Rime's office, for disruptive behavior. Mr. Rime would often give her encouraging pep talks. After hearing LaMonica's conversations, he saw some potential in her. He often referred to her as "Kiddo."

"Alright Kiddo, return to class and be the student I know you can be." Mr. Rime would say.

LaMonica wanted to be that student for Mr. Rime, but try as she might, it just didn't work out. For one thing, the classes were so huge, LaMonica found it hard not to get distracted, especially if it was a subject that she wasn't particularly interested in like math or science. The overhead lights seemed to charge her into overdrive. The next thing she knew she would be up out of her seat re-enacting stories she chose to tell someone across the room and kicked out of class yet again.

Ruby didn't have the same problems that LaMonica had, however. She only felt awkward at school. Staying focused and in control of herself was not a problem for her. So Ruby was not a disruptive student.

Eventually LaMonica ditched the classes she didn't know how to handle. She began skipping school with random people she would find in the bathrooms. The school aides would catch everyone in the restroom and send them to the assistant principal's office.

Now instead of being in Mr. Rime's office for disruptive behavior, she was there almost every day for truancy, one of his "regulars."

"That's it, Kiddo. I'm going to have to call Mrs. Powers. I can't just keep turning a blind eye to you skipping classes."

"Wait, Mr. Rime, please," LaMonica pleaded. She knew she could explain what was going on with her better in writing than speech. "Let me write you a letter."

Mr. Rime agreed. He had some other kids he had to see regarding fights and suspected gang activity. He wanted to nip that in the bud before it got started at South Junior High, so he gave LaMonica paper and pencil while she wrote the letter outside of his office.

When Mr. Rime was ready for LaMonica to present her letter, he was floored. LaMonica had watched him while he read it, waiting for a look of surprise on his face. People usually realized the intelligence she held when they read anything she had written. This usually took them by surprise because of how often her behavior didn't line up with her potential.

Mr. Rime had that surprised look. "Wow, Kiddo! I'm impressed. Now if you'd put this much effort into your schoolwork and studies, you'd be in my office a lot less often."

He and LaMonica both nodded and smiled in agreement.

"Listen, Kiddo. I'm going to send you back to your next class. I need you to let the LaMonica shine who wrote me this letter. Can you do that?"

"Yes, Mr. Rime." LaMonica would try.

LaMonica began giving classes her best effort. Mr. Rime believed in her, and she did not want to disappoint him. She tried to find things about school that she could look forward to. Like the fact that some of her classes rotated every six weeks and she wouldn't be stuck in them for long if she didn't like them.

Finally, one of LaMonica's classes rotated to Spanish class. She was looking forward to that. Mr. Gutierrez taught

Spanish. Even though Spanish was his main course, he seemed to be very interested in photography. All along the walls were pictures of girls. Young girls. Mainly young White girls. Monica ended up in that Spanish class with LaMonica. She leaned over and whispered to her.

"My mom came in here during orientation to meet who would teach Spanish class. When she saw all these pictures on the wall she came back and told me. 'Never stay after class in Spanish. Ever!'"

LaMonica and Monica just glanced at each other. They looked at Mr. Gutierrez. He was always laughing and joking with the White girls. He even seemed to be involved in knowing about their personal lives—who broke up with who? How did their last date go? Etc. etc. They made a mental note, *don't ever stay after class.*

Formal Spanish was a lot harder than LaMonica had imagined it to be. The Spanglish that Luchie's family had taught her made it seem like learning Spanish was going to be a walk in the park. Quite the opposite. Learning Spanish was much more complicated than throwing out some romantic sounding words here and there that suited the situation. You had to understand the difference between masculine and feminine words, how to conjugate verbs, when to use formal words or less formal words, and of course pronunciation and enunciation of the language. And those were just the easy rules. LaMonica kept her head in the books to earn a high grade in Spanish. She averaged around an A- to a B.

What LaMonica didn't understand was that in the teachers' lounge, teachers talked, and they passed along information about students. LaMonica had been one of the students who was "discussed" in the lounge room, and Mr. Gutierrez had heard an earful. He had already determined that no matter how much "potential" Mr. Rime thought she had; she would not disrupt his class. He would not be the one to put up with what other teachers had put up with from her. It would suit him just fine if she skipped his class altogether.

One day during lunch hour, LaMonica and Ruby had gotten caught outside during the rain. When they came back in, they were thoroughly soaked. Spanish class was immediately after. While in the hallway, some of the White kids were swinging their hair and wetting each other up while laughing. This was too much impulsive fun for LaMonica to pass up. She joined in with them. They were all cracking up with laughter as they entered Spanish class. Most of the kids began settling down as class was starting. LaMonica had to do it just one more time. She got up from her seat and swung her wet hair at one of the students she had been playing in the halls with moments before. They laughed and everyone who had been doing it earlier started up again. This sent Mr. Gutierrez into a tirade.

"Sit down! Now!" He yelled out in class. Everyone sat down quickly. Mr. Gutierrez's voice was firm, and he did not give the appearance of a man who messed around. He came straight over to LaMonica's desk, bent over her, put his hand on her desk and despite being in close proximity to her—he began yelling directly in her face.

"Look, don't think I haven't heard about you and all your antics. I've already got your number. You **will not** come into my class disrupting it or riling up good students. Grab your things and get out of my class **now!**"

LaMonica paused. She opened her mouth to explain or at least apologize, but Mr. Gutierrez would hear none of it.

"Now!" He said again while pointing towards the door.

Mr. Gutierrez hadn't given her any specific instructions as to where to go. Nor had she been allowed to ask. When some teachers kicked students out of the class, they wanted them to stand in the hall outside the door. That didn't appear to be his instructions. Sometimes when students were kicked out, they were sent to the office, but they always had an accompanying note with them. He had given her no such note. Honestly, this suited LaMonica just fine. She didn't want to have to give Mr. Rime a disappointing note anyhow.

On a whim, LaMonica decided since she hadn't been given any instructions she would **leave, leave.** She exited the building. LaMonica hurriedly ran until the building was no longer in her sight when she turned around. As she made her way through the neighborhood near South, she saw some students she recognized. They were known as "the stoner kids." LaMonica ran and caught up with "the stoner kids."

They were all smoking cigarettes. "What are you doing out here?" One of them asked.

"I just got kicked out," LaMonica reported.

"Ah man, that sucks dude. Do you want a cigarette?"

"Sure." LaMonica took the cigarette and one of the "stoner kids" lit it for her. Even though she wasn't technically a cigarette smoker, she wasn't new to it either. Most of Luchie's adult siblings smoked Marlboros and Cool cigarettes. Sometimes she and LaMonica would sneak a few out of their packs and smoke them upstairs in the window. Honestly, this was a pastime that only made LaMonica feel excited about rebelling against rules. She didn't enjoy it like Luchie did.

"Where are you guys going?"

"We're headed down to Nicks store. We've got an older friend who's going to meet us and buy beer and cigarettes for us. Do you want to come?"

"Sure." She didn't have anywhere else to be. LaMonica walked down to Nicks smoking right along with the "stoner kids."

Once they arrived she gave her money to the adult that was "helping" minors get cigarettes and drinks. LaMonica opted out of getting any alcohol and just got a pack of cigarettes. They were only $2.75. She still had $2 left over from her weekly lunch money, and one of the other kids gave her the money to cover the rest.

LaMonica and the other kids stayed near the store and chatted. Most of them were into skateboarding and rock music. She found common ground with them in skateboarding. That was something she and Luchie had often enjoyed. LaMonica was pretty good at it for an amateur. She noticed kids yelled out "freaking A" in conversation a lot. Especially when they talked about doing jumps on ramps with their skateboards.

She continued hanging out with them until the end of the day. Once they started seeing students walking home from South, they knew school was out. LaMonica felt nauseated from smoking cigarettes all afternoon. This was definitely not something she would want to do every day.

Despite being nauseated, LaMonica ran hurriedly to catch the bus and headed home like she had been in school all day. Mama had received a phone call at work from the school letting her know LaMonica was in school for the first half of the day but not the second. She came home from work early so she could be there when LaMonica arrived home.

When LaMonica turned the doorknob and walked down the hall Mama was in the living room pacing. Waiting on her.

"You smell like nothing but smoke, LaMonica!" Mama said with a tone that meant she means business.

"Bring yo' ass over here!"

"I'm about to light yo' tail up."

The next thing LaMonica knew, Mama was hitting her all over the place with a switch. She spoke to her on beat with every hit.

"Didn't I (whoosh) tell you (whoosh) to take yo' ass to school (whoosh) and get yo' lesson out (whoosh) and not get in trouble (whoosh, whoosh, whoosh)?!"

LaMonica's body was on fire from the stings that landed from the green tree limb. She had welts from the switch on her arms, legs, back, everywhere.

She was crying and saying. "Please Mama, please no more. Please."

Mama finally stopped. She let LaMonica go and cry and take a nap before dinner and doing the homework she had from morning classes. After dinner Mama called LaMonica to her.

"Come here, LaMonica. Go in there and get me the alcohol."

LaMonica did as she was told.

Take your clothes off and lay down here and let me put alcohol on these welts on your body. The alcohol burned as Mama was putting it on the fresh whipping wounds. LaMonica shook and moved.

"Ahhh," she yelled.

"Be still now. It won't hurt so much if you let me put the alcohol on you and get the soreness out." Mama was talking to LaMonica in her loving voice now. Mama had done this before. The alcohol was supposed to keep her light skin from showing any marks.

It didn't matter to LaMonica how nice Mama sounded; she was still angry at her on the inside.

"Now if you'd just do what you're supposed to do, Mama wouldn't have to whip you like this LaMonica," Mama explained.

LaMonica rolled her eyes, where Mama couldn't see. She knew better than to say anything back. She just wanted her to hurry up so she could get away from her.

LaMonica went to bed that night thinking about her dad and her real family. She thought about her brothers Chuck and Malcolm, who she had met at the park once. She bet they would love her, and they wouldn't treat her like this.

LaMonica started thinking of more reasons to be angry at Mama. She began to feel resentment towards her in that moment. Resentment for how she whipped her. And bitterness for how she wouldn't let her be around her daddy and other family members.

They wanted to see her. What if something happened to her dad and in all this time Mama wouldn't let her see him? LaMonica decided she would never forgive Mama if something happened to her dad and she never got the chance to know him.

ATTIC ANTICS

I n 8th grade, school began looking up. LaMonica had come to understand the shuffling and changing of classes a little bit better. She also was making more positive friends. Kristina, who lived in Sheridan Park near Uncle Charlie, attended South. She and LaMonica enjoyed each other's company. LaMonica also befriended two students who were bussed from the east side like herself, April and Marie.

April was in a special program called Upward Bound, and she invited LaMonica to join. Upward Bound was held every Saturday at Delta Community College. It was geared towards minority students who had a goal of attending college.

On LaMonica's first day as a guest at Upward Bound with April, she enjoyed it. They made learning fun and hands on. Each week the students received a small stipend for attending and they often took field trips to local Michigan Colleges. LaMonica couldn't believe this, but she actually wanted to spend her Saturdays learning.

One of the directors of the program explained to

LaMonica that to get into Upward Bound she'd have to get a character sheet filled out by at least four of her teachers, and they would have to certify that she was passing in their classes.

Some of the teachers who knew LaMonica from 7th grade had remarked on how much more mature she seemed starting off this year. They hoped she would keep up the outstanding work. LaMonica knew if she got the right teachers to fill out her character sheets (the ones who saw her potential) she was a shoe in for Upward Bound.

One of those teachers was Mrs. Tanner. LaMonica was placed in her 8th grade English class and immediately her spark began to shine. Mrs. Tanner was one of those instructors that was passionate about her job. She was also the editor of the school newspaper. Mrs. Tanner saw the potential in LaMonica, and she gave her the opportunity to flourish in writing.

Mrs. Tanner introduced LaMonica to the author, Charles Dickens. The assigned reading of David Copperfield was her favorite. This was the first time she had read a book of this magnitude, the wording was so different, and it was over 1,000 pages long in paperback. LaMonica loved every turn of the page.

At first she was a bit intimidated by such a book, but soon found David's life of rejection relatable. Mrs. Tanner's passion had awakened a spark in LaMonica. She gave each student a journal to write their feelings or thoughts about the current passage they were reading. LaMonica would read several chapters of David Copperfield and write in the journal. Mrs. Tanner would read the journal and respond. She then would ask LaMonica thought provoking questions in the journal for her to respond to. This back and forth invigorated her. Never had LaMonica ever been so excited about a class in her life.

Her excitement spilled over to her other classes. That and the fact that she now had a goal to work towards - stay on the good side of things to remain in Upward Bound. For the first time ever, LaMonica was surrounded by people all working for common positive goals. When her report card came out her grades had improved tremendously. She mainly had A's and B's, because she never skipped class anymore or got thrown out for unacceptable behavior. The teachers couldn't believe the complete turnaround in LaMonica.

LaMonica just knew she had finally earned her freedom to go somewhere from Mama. By 8th grade, LaMonica was still treated like a baby by Mrs. Powers. She would often hear the other students talk about the movies they had gone to see as a group. Or how they had all went and hung out at a restaurant as long as they were back by their curfew. LaMonica didn't have a curfew. Heck, she could barely leave the house in the first place. LaMonica knew she had done untrustworthy things in the past, but hadn't she proven herself a year later?

Now that LaMonica was present and accounted for in all of her classes, Danny Navarro had taken notice of her. He began sending her love notes. Danny asked LaMonica for her phone number and she agreed. On the way home on the bus, LaMonica frantically tried to think of what she would say if Mama or Ms. Demona answered the phone when Danny called. She decided she would say he was her science partner, and they had to talk on the phone about their project.

LaMonica hadn't filled Danny in on this plan, nor had she told him she wasn't allowed to have boy phone calls because she was hoping Mama would soon give her that privilege since she had done so much improvement in school. She had even won an award for Most Improved Student.

"Mama, my science partner Danny is going to be calling this evening to go over our science project," LaMonica lied.

"How come you have a boy for a partner? You couldn't partner up with a girl?"

"No Mama, the teacher picks the science partners."

"Alright, as long as y'all are talking about schoolwork and that's it."

LaMonica, Mama and Ms. Demona were in the middle of having dinner when the phone rang. It was Danny, asking for LaMonica.

Mama passed the phone to her and went back to the dinner table. LaMonica stretched the curly phone cord as far as it would reach and left the kitchen to talk in the living room. She tried to chat with Danny as low as she could on the phone, but she knew Mama and Ms. Demona were listening.

For some odd reason, because of the water lines, the washer was situated in apartment two upstairs and the dryer was situated in the kitchen downstairs. Mama went upstairs to the washroom to wash a load of clothes just before LaMonica hung up. While she was gone Ms. Demona took it as her opportunity to give LaMonica an ear full.

"That shole didn't sound like no science project conversation to me."

"Sounds like you call yo' self liken' that boy. You getting' fast around here, ain't you?"

LaMonica knew better than to respond. Besides, Ms. Demona was hurling her nasty attitude at her so fast, she couldn't respond to each comment if she wanted to.

"Yep, looks like it's about to be another situation like when you was running around with your little boyfriend, Juan, last summer while I was out of town. Is Danny your new man now?

"Girl, you're just a little whore like yo' mama. I don't know what Mrs. Powers is gonna do with you.

"Uh, uh, uh." Ms. Demona headed up the stairs.

Mama came back with a load of laundry to fold.

"LaMonica. That wasn't a science project call. Ain't nobody crazy! I done told you time and time again, you ain't old enough to be courtin' no boys. That boy is not to call here again! Do you understand me?"

"But Mama, my other friends can talk to boys on the phone. Can't I get phone calls even if I don't go out with boys, please?"

"First of all, I don't care what anybody else's parents are letting them do. You ain't doin' it!

"Don't have that boy call here again, LaMonica. **Do you understand me?**"

"Yes ma'am," LaMonica replied.

LaMonica retreated sadly to her room. There just was no freedom for her to do anything, anywhere. She felt so jailed and caged in. She slammed stuff around in her room out of anger.

Mama instantaneously responded.

"Look girl, you don't pay no bills around here. Don't you slam nothin' around in this house. I'm not far off yo' tail."

LaMonica just didn't have an outlet period.

When she went back to school Danny had made her a key in metal shop class. He told her to use it with a stud for an earring in her ear. LaMonica loved it because it looked just like the earring Janet Jackson wore on the Let's Wait Awhile video.

Even closer to that video scenario was the fact that he had found them a secret meeting place up on the roof. They made plans to meet there with another couple for lunch.

LaMonica, Danny and the other couple (Abdul and Rosa) met up on the roof and spent the entire lunch hour together. After lunch time, LaMonica and Rosa went back to the roof.

Rosa was a troubled child, somewhat like LaMonica. Currently, she was in foster care. Both of them were trying to escape something that they each couldn't identify. Going back up to the rooftop after lunch meant LaMonica would be skipping classes again. *I don't care. Mama has already proven that even if I do well in school and get good grades, I still won't get the type of freedom other teenagers get anyway,* LaMonica thought. LaMonica decided she would have to take her freedom where she could get it. At school. She felt she had no choice.

The rooftop was two tiered. There were classrooms on one tier overlooking the rooftop. Because it had recently snowed the rooftop was slushy. LaMonica and Rosa began slip and sliding on one level of the roof. This sent the kids in classes into excitement. They were all in the windows laughing and waving at them. Nobody could figure out how in the world they had gotten up there. None of the staff at South knew how to get up to the roof.

Next Rosa and LaMonica continued their exploring and they found an entrance to the school's attic as well as the overhead to gym class. They began swinging the fluorescent lights over the gym while physical ed was in session. The gym teacher didn't know what to make of it. Then Rosa started throwing insulation down on them. The teacher ended gym class early not knowing what to do.

LaMonica and Rosa retreated back to the attic. Soon

they heard Mr. Rime calling their names over the loud-speaker. He had checked attendance and also spoken with Danny and Abdul. And he knew it was them up there. Mr. Rime demanded that they come down now!

By this time LaMonica and Rosa were covered in insulation filth. Now that everyone knew it was them, there was no way they were coming down until everyone was gone.

Rosa and LaMonica waited the staff and students out. When everyone had left for the day they came down. They were itchy and completely covered in insulation. They decided to walk home in the dark. But when they went to open the doors they were locked. They tried every door in the building. It was useless, they were locked inside until someone opened up the building in the morning.

By this time adventure had turned to hunger. They had no money for the vending machines and nothing to eat. Rosa was super resourceful, she suggested they go to the cooking class and eat. Rosa broke the window in the cooking class door, and they made their way inside. Unfortunately no real food had been left there, just some baking sized bags of M&M's. They ate those and chilled for a while.

Suddenly they heard someone trying to unlock the school doors, so they hurried and ran back into the attic. Rosa suggested they lie down and cover themselves in insulation so they couldn't be spotted. LaMonica did as she directed.

Eventually they heard helicopters on the roof overhead using bullhorns and calling Rosa and LaMonica's name. They continued laying hidden in the attic, covered up in insulation. LaMonica thought maybe they should go out there now that things had escalated to this level, but Rosa said it was a bad idea.

There was a whole rescue team involved now. The

school had called in the construction company that had originally worked on the attic and roof to help out. The construction workers walked throughout the attic shining flashlights, but they couldn't find Rosa and LaMonica hidden in the corner covered up.

Then Rosa's foster parents and Mrs. Powers came into the school at nightfall with the police and bullhorns. Mrs. Powers pleaded with LaMonica over the bullhorn to come down. Rosa and LaMonica heard some construction workers tell the rescue crew that they had recently been working on the roof and attic, and there was a drop off in the attic. They believed LaMonica and Rosa had possibly fallen into it and could be hurt.

LaMonica hated the fact that Mama thought something bad had happened to her, but Rosa continued to advise against them going down. They would have to wait until morning.

When they awoke in the morning, they were too late to go down without the school seeing them, but they had begun to itch from the insulation so reluctantly they went down into the school.

The bell rang just as they were walking down the hall. Everyone was laughing and pointing at how filthy they were from the insulation.

Mr. Rime couldn't save LaMonica this time. The main principal grabbed LaMonica and choked her for speaking with an attitude.

"Do you know how much money and resources were spent on you last night? When I think of the liability, you've cost this school—at least have the decency to have a sorrowful attitude!" The main principal said this after he had cupped his hand around LaMonica's neck and threw her up against the wall. LaMonica promptly sat down and quietly waited for Mama to arrive back at the school at that point.

LaMonica and Rosa were informed that they were expelled. They had to get special permission from the Board of Education to return to school, and even then it wouldn't be until months later in the new year.

Upon her return to school, they promptly tested her for Special Education. To everyone's shock, LaMonica tested above her grade level in many subjects. In English, she tested at a beginning college level. The question lingered—why was she so bad?

Mrs. Powers didn't know what she was going to do with LaMonica at this point. She had sent LaMonica to the best schools, that didn't help. She had enlisted the help of Ms. Demona, that didn't help. Frankly, LaMonica had become the embarrassment to the family. Her own brother thought so. His kids were well behaved and would never try anything like this.

14

"REAL" FAMILY

At this point, Mrs. Powers decided maybe it was time to let LaMonica's father be in her life. Somebody had to help get her straight.

Mama started making statements to LaMonica like, "Maybe your daddy can do something with you."

Mrs. Powers knew where LaMonica's father lived. She decided to pay him a visit.

Chuck Price was quite surprised to see Mrs. Powers at the door.

"I'd like to talk to you about LaMonica if you have a moment, Chuck."

"Come on in, Mrs. Powers."

"LaMonica is out of hand with me. She's running around with boys, getting expelled from school. She even had the helicopters looking for her while she was in the tunnels inside the school. I don't know what to do with her. It seems like it's time for me to let her father step into her life and help out."

Chuck didn't like the fact that the only way he could get close to his daughter was to be a disciplinarian for all the problems LaMonica was into. But he had long wanted to be in his daughter's life, so he decided he would take what he could get.

"Just tell me what to do, Mrs. Powers. I can come pick LaMonica up anytime you want me to.

"I'm off work this weekend do you want me to come pick her up then?"

"Yes, that will be fine," Mama said.

"But I want to warn you, you will need to watch her. Don't let her get on the phone with no boys. She'll try that. She'll try all kinds of stuff. She's gotten mighty fast."

Mama stayed for a while longer and complained to Chuck about his daughter. About how horrible she'd been in school through the years, and about her disrespectful attitude lately.

"I've done all I can to raise her right, Chuck, but despite all that, LaMonica just won't act right. I even let a woman come live in the apartment upstairs to help straighten her out, Demona. She said LaMonica is a disrespectful child. A lost cause because of who her mother is."

"Well, I'm gonna try to help you with her, Mrs. Powers."

When Mama got done talking about LaMonica, Chuck thought to himself, *Mrs. Powers made LaMonica sound almost scary to be around.* This was working on his anxiety. He wasn't sure if she was a child he could handle. But he decided he wanted to meet his problem child for himself.

"Mrs. Powers, LaMonica has my blood in her too. And I believe that's what's gonna help her not be crazy like her mama. Plus Angie was fine until somebody put something in her drink."

Chuck and his family had been waiting for years for the chance to be in LaMonica's life. When he told his mother and his sisters the good news, they were all excited. But they had some reservations.

"Chuck, are you sure this time?" Bren, Chuck's sister, asked.

"I still remember that time she said we could come by when they were living over on Moton Drive and Mrs. Powers wouldn't let you in."

It happened back when LaMonica was just a toddler. Chuck had just got done fighting Mrs. Powers for custody of LaMonica. They didn't have DNA test back in the 70s, so the courts needed Angie to come and verify that Chuck was actually LaMonica's father, but Angie never showed up.

After waiting for a year for Angie to either straighten up or sign papers that Chuck was LaMonica's father, the court ruled in Mrs. Powers' favor. He had fought hard, but the Judge didn't like the fact that Chuck had several other children with outstanding child support. He noted that this helped him also to rule in Mrs. Powers' favor.

Chuck had caught up to Mrs. Powers after court in the parking lot, pleading with her.

"Mrs. Powers, please let me be in my daughter's life."

"You heard the judge Chuck, he said it was up to me and I don't think it would be good for LaMonica to be confused about me being her mama and you being her daddy."

"You could tell her I'm her uncle, anything. Please, Mrs. Powers."

Chuck's sisters had come and were by his side at this point.

Mrs. Powers wasn't afraid of anybody, but she had heard how one of his sisters could get and she didn't want to have to handle her out here at the courthouse where she had just won her case. Plus, agreeing was probably the only thing that was going to make Chuck's pleading stop. So she agreed they could stop by.

Chuck went home thinking he could at least be an uncle in LaMonica's life and that one day he would tell her the truth. He went shopping with his sisters and bought LaMonica (a toddler) a fur coat as a present.

Chuck thought very highly of himself. He had been blessed with the gift of singing. His girlfriend often referred to him as "James" for James Brown, because he could perform all James Brown's dances and songs. Chuck felt because of his good looks and his talent for singing people were often jealous of him.

He could often be heard stating, "I'm the greatest man in the world." In his mind he was the greatest, so that made his kids the greatest too. If he was going to buy them a gift it was going to be top notch.

When Chuck and his sister arrived at Mrs. Powers' house to bring LaMonica the fur coat, Mrs. Powers wouldn't open the door. He could hear LaMonica inside, crying from all the commotion.

"Mrs. Powers, please, I just want to give LaMonica this beautiful coat. I just want to see her like we talked about."

He kept knocking over and over again, and Mrs. Powers tried to quiet LaMonica. Bren and Chuck could hear Mrs. Powers saying, "shhh."

Finally, they left. Chuck didn't take rejection well. That scene would play out in his mind repeatedly for years.

Chuck saved the coat, hoping to one day give it to LaMonica. He had another child by LaMonica's mother named Ambrosia. Ambrosia wasn't quite a full year behind LaMonica. Angie had moved to Detroit and Ambrosia lived with her. A few years later she brought Ambrosia to visit in the middle of the winter and the child wasn't wearing a coat.

Chuck gave the fur coat he had saved to her. Angie immediately disappeared back to Detroit with the child after that,
and no one had seen Ambrosia since.

LaMonica's father came and picked her up that weekend.
He came inside the big yellow house and introduced
himself.

"I'm yo' daddy. We're gonna be getting to know a lot
about each other. I've missed you. I love you hear? And yo'
family loves you too."

LaMonica called him Daddy right away. "I love you too,
Daddy."

She was so excited she was finally going to get to spend
time with her dad. When she got into the car, she met
Daddy's girlfriend and stepdaughter.

"Hi, I'm Linda, your daddy's girlfriend. This is my
daughter, Tondra."

Tondra was almost the same age as LaMonica.

LaMonica was so delighted to be spending time with
Daddy, his girlfriend Linda, and her new stepsister Tondra.

The car they were riding in was so cool. It was nicer than
anything Mama had ever had. His car was called a New
Yorker. It was shiny and it had voice commands. If the door
was left open it said, "The door is ajar, the door is ajar."
Daddy worked at the GM Plant, so he had that plant money,
and he could afford things like that.

As they were riding down the street, he began
explaining to LaMonica what they were going to be doing
for the day.

"Today is your grandma's birthday. We're having a

birthday celebration over there and some of your brothers are already there."

"Okay Daddy, you mean Malcolm and Chuck will be there?"

"Yes, and your brother Teddy just moved back to Saginaw from Louisiana, he's coming by too."

This made LaMonica feel so much better about going into a new atmosphere. True, she had been wanting to be around her dad for a long time, but she really didn't know him. Chuck and Malcolm, she already knew and loved.

LaMonica knew who her brothers Chuck and Malcolm were because their mother used to come around when she was little, and eventually Mama let her visit with them. Chuck and Malcolm had the same mother. Daddy had children by multiple women. Some women he had children in sets with, like Chuck and Malcolm or her older two brothers, Brynner and Alvin and LaMonica and her sister Ambrosia. Altogether Daddy had 7 children by 4 different women.

Chuck and Malcolm were mixed like LaMonica and Ambrosia. Birdie was their mother. From the time LaMonica was little, Mama had allowed Birdie to drop in every now and again. She would get pictures from Mama and take them back to Chuck and his family. Eventually Mrs. Powers allowed LaMonica to go to Birdie's and visit with her brothers on some late nights when she worked the bingo and Ms. Demona wasn't available. So LaMonica was very familiar with Chuck and Malcolm.

They made it to LaMonica's grandma's house. Her paternal grandmother, Ceceil, was very glad to see her. She was filled with tears and had long hugs and stories for LaMonica.

"I remember the day you were born. I was there. You were so beautiful with silky black hair.

"I used to keep you too, you know. Yo' mama, Angie had run off somewhere, but I had you with me. Me and your daddy were taking care of you together—when out of nowhere Mrs. Powers showed up with the police and social workers and took you from us."

"Yes. I wanted you," Daddy explained. "Mrs. Powers had just gotten attached to you from babysitting you and she took you from me," Daddy continued.

LaMonica had never heard this part of the story. She would have to ask Mama about this later. These secrets Mama kept were making her distrust Mama because she had always been honest with her as far as she knew.

As the party started picking up everyone started segmenting themselves off into their own groups. Grandma Ceceil loved playing Pokeno. She had a table going with a few friends. Daddy had oldies music playing, and he was singing. Her brothers Chuck and Malcolm were singing along with Daddy as back up. The atmosphere was one of happiness and fun.

Everyone was drinking including her two brothers Chuck and Malcolm who were even younger than her. Apparently her dad let them openly drink alcohol. More family members piled into the grandmother's small apartment. LaMonica finally met another one of her brothers, Teddy. He had just moved back to Michigan from down south.

Everyone was having a great time, but LaMonica's dad didn't allow her or her stepsister to drink alcohol. All the brothers and male cousins were drinking beer while they played oldies music and made jokes. Grandma Ceceil didn't drink alcohol. She actually sung in a gospel group. But she didn't have a problem with her son celebrating her birthday this way either. LaMonica observed that it seemed like it was probably the norm.

Suddenly a fight broke out between LaMonica's cousin Beau and her brother Teddy. Apparently they both liked the same girl that attended the party and were fighting over her. LaMonica's dad took her brother's side and her cousin Beau started cussing out her dad. They dragged Beau out of the apartment, cussing and wanting to fight Teddy.

This whole scenario just reminded LaMonica of every bad thing she had ever heard of her father's side of the family. Mama and Ms. Demona had always said they liked to drink and party and fight. Here she was watching it play out right before her very eyes, on day one.

On the drive home Daddy warned her, "Don't tell Mrs. Powers what happened tonight, or she won't let me come get you anymore."

"Okay Daddy, I won't." LaMonica thought, *I'm not about to tell Mama anything, hasn't she kept secrets herself?*

When Daddy pulled into the driveway he wanted to make sure LaMonica understood how much she was loved, wanted and accepted.

"LaMonica I want you to understand. I think a lot of myself. I'm handsome, I can sing, and I've got long pretty hair. I think I'm the greatest man in the world. Now if I think I'm the greatest thang there is, what do you think I feel about my kids?"

"Yeah." LaMonica responded.

"Don't ever think that your family didn't want you. I had you when you were a little baby and Mrs. Powers came and took you from me, because she had got attached to you from when Angie was having her watch you. But I never wanted to give you up. I wanted my baby. Mrs.

Powers wouldn't let me see you in all this time. Okay? I love you."

"Okay Daddy." And with that Daddy gave her a kiss and dropped her back off.

Mama thought everything went fine, so she agreed to let LaMonica go back to Chuck's house the following weekend.

Daddy and his girlfriend came and picked her up again for the weekend, and she was excited to be spending the night with her new stepsister, Tondra. Everyone was so nice to her at Daddy's house. He had a small ranch style home, but it was nicely furnished. Not like Mama, who got everything from the rummage sale. His stuff was brand new. It was expensive, and it was very obvious how important his things were to him and that they be clean and perfect.

LaMonica, being a combination of messy and clumsy, hoped she could keep his things the way he liked it. Linda and Tondra were super nice to LaMonica, while daddy was shuffling around getting ready for work.

Chuck worked third shift. Before he left out the door he came in to tell LaMonica and Tondra good night. The girls were having such a good time that they were laughing and joking in bed when they were supposed to be falling asleep. Daddy came in jokingly saying, "Who's still up making noises and jokes in here?" LaMonica giggled and said, "That's not me Daddy, that's Tondra. She keeps telling me something funny and making me laugh."

Daddy laughed. He was happy to see his daughter so happy at his home.

He gave LaMonica a kiss on the cheek. "I'm leaving for work. I'll see you tomorrow." It didn't seem like it was his regular routine to kiss his stepdaughter on the cheek, and he did not.

As soon as he was gone LaMonica's new stepmother,

Linda came into the bedroom and said, "LaMonica it seems like you want James to like you more than he likes Tondra. Don't think I didn't catch that!"

LaMonica had no idea what she was talking about.

The next day on Saturday, Tondra's friends came over to visit. They all sat at the table in the kitchen. Linda was gone running errands and Daddy was sleeping from working third shift.

"It must be real messed up to be mixed. I mean to be half White is just so nasty," Tondra said.

LaMonica could not believe her ears. Her heart sunk.

Tondra's friends chimed in.

"Girl, I know. I bet you when her hair gets wet she smells like a wet dog too," one of Tondra's friends added.

All the girls erupted into laughter. LaMonica couldn't take it! Out of nowhere Birdie pulled up to drop her two brothers Chuck and Malcolm off. As the boys ran into the house LaMonica was running out. They didn't notice that she was upset. By the time LaMonica made it to the car to talk to Birdie, she was in tears. She was crying and begging Birdie to please take her with her.

"Please take me with you! Please I'm begging you, please."

"What happened LaMonica?"

"Tondra is in there making fun of me for being half White and for being mixed. All her friends are laughing at me and calling me names. I just want to go. Please, can you take me with you?"

"Why don't you tell your dad what's going on?" Birdie asked.

"He's sleep from working." Plus, honestly, LaMonica didn't know how to talk to Daddy about things like that.

"Well, tell Linda when she gets back."

LaMonica was so hurt and upset. All she wanted to do was jump in the car with Birdie and get out of there. She explained how Linda had acted the night before. Birdie continued with other options.

"But your brothers are here now. Tell them. They need to see Linda and Tondra for who they really are. Then they can tell your dad."

LaMonica quickly assessed that Birdie was suggesting that LaMonica sit there and let them spew more hate at her in the hopes that her brothers would observe it as witnesses. LaMonica had no interest in being an emotional guinea pig for this experiment.

"No, I don't want to wait for that. Please, just let me go with you now, please." LaMonica and Birdie had an emotional connection. They had developed a sort of mother/daughter relationship. Birdie was this way with most of Daddy's kids. LaMonica trusted her much more than being at Daddy's house right now.

"Fine." Birdie saw the hurt in LaMonica's eyes and gave in. She blew the horn and Tondra came to the door. "Tell Chuck when he wakes up I took LaMonica with me."

Birdie took LaMonica to a movie and then dropped her back off at home with Mama. LaMonica didn't dare tell Mama how horribly she had been treated behind her dad's back at his house. She still wanted to be able to visit with him. She would just have to be careful around his girlfriend and his stepdaughter.

When Birdie's sons Chuck and Malcolm returned home from spending the weekend at their dad's she informed them of how LaMonica had been treated. Birdie asked Mrs. Powers to bring LaMonica over to her house to spend time with her brothers. While there visiting Chuck and Malcolm had a talk with LaMonica and they told her don't go over there unless they are there too.

"Tondra is just jealous of you LaMonica because you're pretty. She's really jealous of all of us. Her and her mama. See me and Malcolm, we usually go over there together, and we have each other's back. If you go there alone, there's nobody to have your back. So make sure you only go over to Daddy's house when at least one of us is there. No matter how nice they act to you always remember they really don't like you, because they really don't like us. They are jealous of all of us because we're Daddy's real kids."

LaMonica understood now. She had never seen anything like this before. She had never been in the middle of a stepfamily situation, but she surmised it was a hard circumstance to be in. Never would she have imagined she'd have to be this strategic to see her own father.

LaMonica did as her brothers advised her and only went to visit her father when her brothers were also going. She would wait until they had made it over there, and then they'd call, and she would have Mama drop her off from that point forward.

15

NOW EVERYBODY'S GETTING TIPSY

One weekend when they were all there visiting watching movies, Chuck, Malcolm, LaMonica and Tondra asked to be dropped off at the mall. To LaMonica's surprise, Daddy dropped them off. This was a freedom that LaMonica had never enjoyed as a teenager (going to the mall without a parent).

As soon as she stepped in, she had the attention of the guys her age there. Immediately they started running up to her, asking her for her phone number. LaMonica's brothers quickly stepped in front of each and everyone, trying to "holler" at her. "No, that's my sister. She don't want your number and you can't have hers."

LaMonica thought it was nice to be watched over like this and cared about by her brothers.

As time passed LaMonica continued to visit with her brothers and her dad on the weekends and sometimes after school or whenever school was closed. She loved the fact that she didn't have to be around mean Ms. Demona hardly ever anymore. Nor did she have to be around Mama that much and her extra overprotective ways.

Every weekend Daddy would rent movies like Super Fly and all kinds of old school Black movies that LaMonica had never seen before. Daddy and LaMonica's brothers would drink beers while they all sat around and joked. And then slowly but surely Daddy started getting a little more lax and letting LaMonica have a beer too.

Daddy's philosophy was that if he allowed his kids to drink with him, at least he knew their drinks were safe and no one had put anything in them. Daddy was overly anxious about a lot of things, and one of them was that someone would one day try to put something in his drink or the people he cared about drinks. For this reason, he didn't believe in public bars or parties outside of being with family. He felt by letting his children drink at home with him; he was doing them a favor and keeping them safe.

LaMonica engaging in underage drinking is just the nightmare dilemma that Mama had always fought to avoid. If she knew this was going on, she would lose it.

LaMonica's behavior began improving in school. Now that she had an outlet, she no longer felt the need to skip school anymore. Mama had learned from the counselor it was best to extend privileges to LaMonica when her behavior warranted it, so she could get more of that behavior from her. Mama extended these privileges to include LaMonica visiting her cousins on her father's side as well.

She still didn't like to leave LaMonica alone on Friday nights when she worked late night at the bingo so sometimes she would drop her off at either her brother's house or her father's house (LaMonica would only request to go over there if her brothers were there too). Sometimes LaMonica would visit with her father's sister Bren and her sons. She had gotten really close with her cousin Beau.

One Friday when Mrs. Powers dropped LaMonica off at her cousin Beau's house unbeknownst to her, Beau was having a party. Mrs. Powers was in a hurry to make it to work and didn't see LaMonica off to the inside. It's a good thing she didn't because she would have seen young teens inside drinking. LaMonica's Aunt Bren was gone to the bingo hall to play bingo where Mama worked, so she had no idea that this party was going on either.

When LaMonica arrived at Beau's house she told him she had a sore throat so he gave her some beer and told her that would help. She kept drinking the beer, but her throat remained sore.

"Beau, it's not helping," she said.

Beau handed LaMonica some 80 Proof liquor and said, "Here drink this. You ain't gonna have a sore throat no more - because you're gonna be drunk." Beau whispered that last part.

LaMonica had never had liquor before. The strongest thing she had ever had was wine coolers and beer until that point. The liquor burned going down her throat and she couldn't drink it, so she began mixing it with beer so it went down easier. This really "tore her up." Meaning she was quickly becoming intoxicated.

While LaMonica was becoming intoxicated, more and more of Beau's friends began to pile into the house and they were bringing drinks with them. LaMonica's brothers arrived. They did not like the state she was in, especially with so many dudes in the house. They were in full on protection mode and heavily guarded her.

Soon all that alcohol took effect and LaMonica was completely inebriated. After a while, her brothers were starting to have a good time with the company and were no longer paying her as much attention as before. She mentioned to Beau that her mother would be off work soon.

"We've got to get you sobered up before she gets here then," Beau said.

He took LaMonica into the bathroom and put her in the shower, wetting her hair, clothes, everything. Beau did this despite the fact that LaMonica had just come from the hair salon the day before and this ruined her hairstyle.

Her brothers realized she was gone from the main area of company and came and found her. They didn't like the look of what they saw going on and they said, "No, we've got her." They pulled her out of there and just had her putting water on her face, trying to get her sober before Mrs. Powers made it back.

When Mrs. Powers made it back LaMonica was still completely inebriated. Mrs. Powers was heated.

"Who gave my daughter this amount of alcohol? Who gave her any alcohol at all?"

Beau would only stammer with no real answers. Mrs. Powers grabbed LaMonica, put her in the car and took her to her father's house. LaMonica remained in the car while Mama knocked on the door. Chuck stepped outside.

"Come look at what your nephew has done to your daughter," Mama said.

LaMonica hopped out of the car. She was talking out of her head. She was cussing and obviously completely drunk.

"Do you see what your nephew did to my daughter? She's completely drunk! Do you see this?" Mrs. Powers went on.

"I'm not drunk, Daddy. She's lyin'. I'm not drunk," LaMonica's said while stammering out of the car and slurring her words like a sloppy drunkard. She must have been drunk to ever call Mama a liar to her face.

"She's lyin' Daddy. Don't believe her," she said again.

Chuck Price thought it was cute and funny the way LaMonica was acting. It took everything in him not to laugh. Later he would joke with her and her brothers about this.

"I'm sorry, Mrs. Powers. I had no idea my nephew would give her liquor like that. I'm so sorry."

"Well, she won't be going over there no more," Mrs. Powers said.

Little did Mama know LaMonica had drinks at her dad's house all the time. Just not *that* much.

Soon after that, LaMonica took part in a survey at school that asked about alcohol use and drug use. LaMonica had never used any drugs, but she had sure enough had a lot to drink thanks to Daddy and his family. She answered the questions sincerely.

Everyone who answered the questions honestly about alcohol or drugs were called into the counseling office and given a referral for counseling at the Health Department.

Mama took LaMonica to a Black counselor at the Health Department who specialized in substance abuse and alcohol, but honestly she just listened to LaMonica gab on and on every session, with no input and not much advice. The only significant input LaMonica could remember the counselor giving her was on their New Year's Eve follow up appointment. LaMonica came back to her counseling appointment and told of her drinking stories. Her reply was, "Yeah, I was thinking about you on New Year's Eve. I know how Black people like to use drinking as a way to celebrate." That was it. That was the full scope of the alcohol counseling advice.

16

OKLAHOMA IS NOT OK!

By the time LaMonica was in the 9th grade, Mama had started getting some serious phone calls from her family in Oklahoma. They had long left Mississippi and had lived in Oklahoma for years now. The family began calling, saying that Mrs. Powers' father was sick.

LaMonica had always loved her grandfather. He was a kind man. He often called the house with joyous laughter. He would always ask to speak directly with LaMonica when he called Mama too. Grandaddy would say, "When you coming down here with Paw Paw? Girl when you come down here Paw Paw is gone take you to the store and buy you some oranges and ice-cream and candy."

He had been doing this ever since LaMonica was a little girl. He just had a heart full of love and joy. Paw Paw reminded LaMonica of Uncle Charlie. They had the same cheerful spirit. Paw Paw's treatment of LaMonica was in direct opposite to the treatment LaMonica had received from her grandmother, his wife.

LaMonica's family often sent their kids to Tulsa, Oklahoma, for the summer to be with their grandmother. One summer LaMonica went. When she got there, it was clear that the grandmother already had her views about her. She did not accept LaMonica as one of the other grandkids. To the point she was often purposely mean to her. Even the other grandkids (LaMonica's cousins) couldn't deny it because it was so blatant.

LaMonica was raised quite differently from the grandmother's other grandchildren. Mama might have seemed strict in LaMonica's eyes, but it was nothing compared to being raised in a true southern Black family way. Kids were to be seen and not heard. They were to never speak out of turn. And they were to obey immediately when corrected. Often LaMonica's southern family would whip all the kids for what one child had done wrong. All of these strict rules were foreign to LaMonica. She generally didn't do well with them because of her impulses (especially speaking out of turn).

One day when the family was all sitting around chatting, LaMonica, desperate for something to read, grabbed the family bible. It had the dates of everyone's birthday written in it. LaMonica saw that Grandma's birthday made her sixteen years old when she had her Uncle Louis.

"Ooh, Grandma! I figured out your age when you had Uncle Louis. You were sixteen. But it says right here y'all didn't get married until *this other* date."

"Gal, you don't know what you're talkin' about. Ain't nobody had no baby before they got married. Oh nawl. We don't believe in that. I don't believe in that, and my husband doesn't either. You don't know what you're talkin' about! You need to just hush your mouth up."

LaMonica certainly wasn't trying to say that, but inadvertently that was what she had done. Being a ten-year-old impulsive child, she didn't know any better. And who knows? She wasn't the best at math, so her calculations were probably off.

From that point forward, LaMonica became the target of the grandmother's deep-seated disdain. If the other grand-kids were going shopping, the grandmother would always say, "No LaMonica can't go." She would do this despite the fact that LaMonica had her own money that Mama had sent with her to Oklahoma.

Another example is when all the cousins were going skating and the grandma said, "No LaMonica can't go." All of LaMonica's cousins chimed in, "Why Grandma. Why can't she go?" They all felt bad that she had missed the last fun event. The grandmother had no valid answer. LaMonica's cousin Joy, who was there with LaMonica from Saginaw, pleaded with the grandma. "Please Grandma, let her go." All the other cousins joined in, pleading with her as well, and so she finally gave in.

Something deep, deep within the grandmother hated LaMonica for being different and looking different. Other people saw it too. Joy saw it. She even mentioned to LaMonica that maybe she could find her real family one day. Paw Paw was a quiet man and didn't argue with his wife during these times. LaMonica often would spend the night at her aunt's house with her other cousins in order to avoid this harsh treatment.

One day when all the cousins were gathered at the grandmother's house, LaMonica was looking through a JCPenney's magazine. She loved flipping through magazines and looking at clothing. Suddenly she saw a pretty mixed model wearing JCPenney's clothes, and she got overly excited (as LaMonica tended to do).

"Grandma, look at this model! Look at this girl in the JCPenney book. She looks just like me!"

LaMonica's grandmother turned to her in anger, grabbed the book from her and said, "That gal don't look nothing like you. Do you understand me? You don't look nothing like her and she don't look nothing like you. You could never be nothing like the girl in this picture."

Some of LaMonica's cousins secretly told her that the grandparents and other relatives had received reports from Mama and Ms. Demona of all the problems LaMonica had been having in school, and so that was why the grand-mother felt the way she did about LaMonica. The atmosphere was so horrible that after Mama found out how LaMonica was being treated; she had her Uncle Louis drive her back early from the summer trip. This was frustrating to Joy because she was happy there in Oklahoma and now her trip had to be cut short because Grandma didn't like LaMonica. As a child, Joy could only have a limited under-standing of how LaMonica felt. All LaMonica knew was she was so happy to be going back home and getting away from that place. She never wanted to go there again.

LaMonica had visited Oklahoma with Mama for vaca-tion about every couple of years prior to that, and she had never received that sort of treatment. But this was her first time going alone. Things had certainly switched up. She vowed she would never go back there again if she had anything to do with it. She didn't want to be treated hateful by people who were supposed to be family but didn't accept her because she looked different, acted different or because she was adopted.

When they returned home, Grandaddy continued to call. LaMonica still had her joyful, quick conversations with him because he had never treated her that way. But Grand-daddy began to call less and less because the cancer had taken a hold of him and he had to be cared for.

Mama called every day to check on Granddaddy. Whenever she couldn't get somebody on the phone, she would freak out and break into tears.

"I'm so concerned about my daddy. I'm just so worried about my daddy," Mama would cry aloud.

This wasn't like her. Mama never cried. LaMonica wasn't used to Mama acting like this, because she had always been a strong, kick your tail type. Mama didn't cry. She walked around ready to bust a cap, carried her pistol and manipulated her way into getting even with those who she determined to be her enemies. But she definitely didn't cry.

Mama was the type to be able to physically handle a situation. LaMonica had even watched her fight a Pit Bull dog (who had been attacking bus riders) and win.

During the day she worked as a home health aide and took care of patients and in the evenings she worked as a security guard keeping other's safe. She just couldn't take feeling helpless and not having a hands on approach to helping her daddy. She was going to want to move to Oklahoma, LaMonica could feel it.

"LaMonica, I can't stay here any longer while my daddy is sick and I don't know what's happening with him. I have to go down to Oklahoma and take care of my daddy. We're gonna have to close up the downstairs and move on down there and take care of Paw Paw."

LaMonica was far too old for a babysitter at this point, but Ms. Demona remained upstairs as Mama's tenant. They had worked out a deal where Ms. Demona did some cleaning and just paid Mama $150 a month in rent. She would be there to watch over the house while they were gone.

LaMonica and her friends from South Junior High wrote each other long goodbye letters so LaMonica would have something to read on the long trip. Mama had not told her how long they would be gone. As far as LaMonica knew this was permanent. The underlying missing information was it would be as long as Granddaddy needed cancer treatment or would be alive, but Mama couldn't bring herself to say that.

There seemed to be no time to tell Daddy that LaMonica was leaving. She called Daddy on the phone right before they left, but he wasn't there to answer and so she had no way to inform him she was moving out of the state. No one in LaMonica's biological family knew what had happened to her or anyone else outside of her school friends. Not Daddy, her brothers, Birdie, no one. Mama packed them up, and they moved to Tulsa, Oklahoma.

Tulsa, Oklahoma, was a very large city compared to the small town of Saginaw that LaMonica was from. The school system was different as well. Back home in Saginaw in 9th grade, LaMonica was still in junior high. But in Tulsa, 9th grade was considered high school.

Mama enrolled LaMonica in the huge sprawling high school for their district. She had to be bussed there as the high school was quite a few miles away from Grandma's house. In comparison, the school was about the size of the community college back home. Attendance was sizable to say the least. There were more pupils in attendance than both of the high schools in Saginaw combined.

LaMonica felt somewhat lost at this school. The curriculum was certainly different. Some classes were much more accelerated than Saginaw Public Schools. In 9th grade, her computer class consisted of her programming computers using algebraic equations. She tried to do the best she could and just focus on English class.

Most of the Black kids were bussed in from Crip gang

neighborhoods. LaMonica found out that the neighborhood the grandmother lived in was considered a Crip hood. Everybody called each other, "cuz" when talking. And there were drive-by shootings in Black neighborhoods on the regular. Even though LaMonica had grown up in the worst neighborhood in Saginaw, it was no match for Crip and Blood gang wars. LaMonica felt like she had stepped into the movie Colors. Oh sure, they had gangs in Saginaw, but nothing syndicated like this.

The White kids pretty much stayed separate from the Black kids. They seemed to have a lot of positivity going on. They participated in things like wrestling and after-school programs. You never heard them running around talking about, "cuz." Or participating in gangs or crimes. The total scene was just very, very different from LaMonica's junior high school.

Of all the family members in Tulsa, LaMonica knew Uncle Louis the best because he was originally from Saginaw. Uncle Louis used to rent one of the apartments upstairs in the big yellow house a long time ago. Now that he had retired from the GM Plant, he moved down to Oklahoma to be near his family.

Uncle Louis had married a woman who was also originally from Saginaw but lived in Tulsa, ironically. Mama's entire family there in Tulsa hated this woman. Some of them seemed to feel the same way about her as they felt about LaMonica. Her name was Aunt Valerie. Aunt Valerie was quite a bit younger than Uncle Louis, and they had just had a baby together. LaMonica's new baby cousin, Lewy. Somehow LaMonica convinced Mama to let her spend a lot of time at Uncle Louis and Aunt Valerie's house, and it was heavenly.

Aunt Valerie was a lot like LaMonica's first counselor.

The one who understood that teenagers have thoughts and feelings, desires, and wants and deserve to be heard and treated like a person. She spent countless hours talking with Aunt Valerie. Aunt Valerie would even share personal things with her. Besides the great friendship LaMonica had with Aunt Valerie, she loved spending time with her new baby cousin Lewy and helping out with him.

Months seemed to whiz by and Granddaddy got worse and worse with the cancer. One day he passed on while LaMonica was at school. When she came home Mama was crying because her daddy was gone.

"He's gone, LaMonica. Daddy is gone," Mama said with tears streaming down her face. They didn't hug because that's not something that Mama and LaMonica really did, but LaMonica wanted to be near her mother and be there for her in the ways that she could.

Everyone from the church that Grandma and Granddaddy and their family attended came by and brought food and beverages so the family didn't have to worry about cooking after Granddad's passing.

On one of the particular days during the mourning period, all the cousins (which were all Grandma's grandkids) were sitting down in a row with legs crossed, watching TV and eating while company came and went. Now company expected for Grandma to have different people in her home since there was a passing, which is the tradition. One visitor, a woman, saw LaMonica amongst the other grandkids and pointed her out.

"Your grandkids are all so nicely behaved, Ms. Agnes. They're all sitting quietly. Are all these your grandchildren? I don't think I've seen this one here before. She's so pretty. What's her name?"

"Who you talking about, girl? You done seen all my grandchildren before," Grandma replied.

"No, not this one." The woman continued pointing until it was obvious she was pointing out LaMonica.

"Her she's so beautiful is this your grandbaby too?"

"Not at all! These is my grandkids," Grandma said while pointing at all the other children. "That one there, that's just a giveaway," she said while referring to LaMonica.

These words stung LaMonica and her mother wasn't home because she was out running errands for the funeral arrangements. LaMonica just cried and cried and cried until Mama came home. As soon as Mama walked in the door LaMonica went into the back bedroom with her and told her what had been said.

Mrs. Powers was furious. She actually broke Black protocol and questioned her mother about it. The grandmother made a lame excuse. She said she wanted to have a talk with LaMonica so they would all have an understanding. The next day LaMonica, Mama and LaMonica's aunt met with the grandmother in the kitchen. LaMonica should have known better than to expect an apology. All the grandmother had was matriarch authority and this lame excuse -

"Now look, I don't know what you think happened, but all that happened is that woman asked me about my grandkids. Now I have to tell the truth. Just like my grandson Thomas, who I raised up. If somebody, ask me if he's my son, I have to tell the truth. He's not my son, he's my grandson. And that's just all I was doing." The grandmother said this in a slow, nicer than normal tone and a drawn out voice. But Mama or LaMonica wasn't buying it.

Mama didn't think of LaMonica as nothing other than her very own daughter. Heck, she had had her since she was two weeks old, basically. That's when Angie started dropping her off for babysitting. Mama was upset. She grabbed all of her and LaMonica's belongings out of her mother's spare bedroom and they promptly moved into LaMonica's aunt's house. After the funeral, LaMonica and Mama moved back to Saginaw and LaMonica couldn't have been happier.

When she made it back to Saginaw, the first thing she did was call her daddy and tell him where she had been.

"I've been driving all around town looking for you, LaMonica. I looked for you at all the different school events. I rode by Mrs. Powers' house everyday looking for you and no one appeared to be home. I was so worried, and I had no idea where you were. Everyone in the family was worried because we didn't know what had happened to you."

The house appeared empty because Ms. Demona had been in a car accident that totaled her car, so no car was ever in the driveway when Daddy rode by. Also, Ms. Demona was much more closed off inside the house than Mama was when she was home. She kept the curtains closed and the front porch door closed, so it always looked like no one was there.

Daddy was so happy he had found LaMonica again. He wanted to come and pick her up right away and she went to visit him. She called her brothers Chuck & Malcolm, and they met her over there. Her father's side of the family was much more affectionate than Mama. Everyone hugged her because they missed her so.

LaMonica also had a couple of surprises waiting for her at Daddy's house. First Linda was pregnant. Daddy would be having his 8th child and LaMonica would be getting a new baby brother or sister. She was very excited about that.

The other surprise was that Linda's daughter, Tondra, was also pregnant at the same time and at just thirteen years old she would soon have a baby too.

17

THE QUEEN MEETS THE BISHOP

L aMonica hooked back up with her friend Lisa from childhood upon her return from Oklahoma. Mama seemed to be much more lax in LaMonica's freedom now that she was fifteen. Of course she still could not do what most teenagers her age could do, but she was being allotted much more freedom than she had before.

On one occasion when Lisa came over for a visit, she was bold enough to ask Mama if she and LaMonica could go on a walk around the neighborhood, which is what Lisa was used to doing in her own free time. Surprisingly enough, Mama agreed. LaMonica was so excited about this because she could rarely go anywhere with friends prior to coming back from Oklahoma.

LaMonica and Lisa walked around 5th and 6th Streets and all the way to the projects. On their way back, they walked down Norman Street to get back to 5th. That's when Lisa spotted her godbrother, Bishop sitting outside on the porch. "Oh, that's my godbrother. Let's go say hi!" Lisa exclaimed.

LaMonica went over to meet Bishop. He seemed nice.

He and Lisa seemed a bit flirtatious and playful with each other. Bishop would pick her up and they would laugh. LaMonica just stood there and observed, not knowing what to think or do. Soon Bishop's brother Alonzo came walking up to the house from the store. It became clear that these two young men lived at the home by themselves. Alonzo was barely an adult and Bishop was maybe a couple of years older than LaMonica. They were both young like LaMonica and Lisa, but they appeared to be living a hard life.

As LaMonica and Lisa were leaving and walking back to the big yellow house, she asked Lisa if she and Bishop liked each other because of their playfulness.

"No, no, that's just my godbrother girl. I don't think he's cute at all. Everybody always used to think his brother Alonzo, the light-skinned one, was the fine one. He still walks bow legged, and that's sexy. But he used to be fine. I don't know what's going on with him now."

Lisa said that Bishop and his brother used to live near her with their mother, and that's how she knew them. Bishop had always been a play godbrother to her. She said since they had been living on their own they had been kind of living a rough life and it showed. Especially on Alonzo because he wasn't fine like he used to be.

Something about Bishop stood out to LaMonica. She couldn't quite put her finger on it, but she was always attracted to the counted out, discounted people of the world. LaMonica put Bishop out of her head and returned to South Junior High School to complete 9th grade.

After returning to South Junior High School in the 9th grade, somehow not all of LaMonica's credits transferred from Oklahoma. Despite Tulsa, Oklahoma's classes being accelerated, she was missing a half a credit to move on to high school in the Saginaw Public School District.

LaMonica along with her good friend Kristina both realized they were missing a half a credit. They were told that along with a few other students they would have to return to South Junior High in the fall for a half a semester instead of moving on to high school.

Both Kristina and LaMonica found that this would be extremely embarrassing for everyone to know that they were supposed to be graduating to 10th grade and yet they were returning to junior high school instead. Kristina devised a plan for them to go to Heritage High School in the Saginaw Township, which is deep in the suburbs. At Heritage, high School began in the 9th grade, so no one would know that LaMonica and Kristina were half a semester behind.

Kristina's mother and LaMonica's mother found people who they knew that were living in the township and didn't mind them using their residential addresses for school. At the time, the Saginaw Township did not accept open enrollment.

Kristina and LaMonica grew closer and closer together because they were the only two that knew each other at this new school. They had very similar appearances, except Kristina was taller with a thinner frame than LaMonica. Both girls were light-skinned with long flowing hair. They looked as if they could have even been related.

They started going over each other's houses frequently, and Kristina even shared some very personal information with LaMonica. She had been hurt by a family member, and her mother had never addressed the situation.

Now that Kristina's mother, Mrs. Belk, was upset with that particular family member, she wanted Kristina to address the wrongdoing that had happened back when she was a young child. Kristina refused to address it. She wasn't emotionally ready. Her mother began leaving flyers on the refrigerator about other children who grew up and reported this family issue and had family members arrested later in life. Mrs. Belk kept urging Kristina to hurry and report it before the statutory time ran out. Kristina's mother seemed bent on revenge and not so much on Kristina's emotional healing.

It was awful because her forceful guidance didn't appear to be done out of a genuine spirit. It was absolutely obvious to LaMonica that Kristina was extremely stressed from all this pressure. So much so that Kristina began getting skinnier and skinnier, and it appeared that she didn't eat much of anything. LaMonica surmised that Kristina didn't want to have to approach the refrigerator and look at these flyers and articles bringing up emotions she wasn't ready to address daily, so she chose not to eat.

One day out of nowhere LaMonica received a visit from Kristina's mother and she was begging LaMonica to tell her where Kristina was. LaMonica had no idea why she hadn't been able to get ahold of Kristina on the phone or hadn't seen her in school, but now she knew.

"I don't know where she is, Mrs. Belk, I swear."

LaMonica was telling the truth. But soon after Mrs. Belk had come by, Kristina began to call and check in with her. LaMonica was the only person who Kristina would check in with. It made her nervous to know that Kristina was somewhere out there and not safe, but she wouldn't dare betray her friend.

Mrs. Belk wouldn't give up. She kept coming by the house pleading and pleading for LaMonica to tell her where her daughter was. But honestly, LaMonica had no idea where Kristina was. She just knew that Kristina was supposedly okay because she checked in with her almost every day, but she absolutely refused to tell even LaMonica where she was located. The only thing she would reveal was that she was with an older guy who drove a tow truck and that she rode along with him when he made his runs.

LaMonica never forgot the desperate looks on Mrs. Belk's face and her quivering voice when she was worried about her daughter. Even though LaMonica often wished to get away from Mama, she never wanted to make her feel the way Mrs. Belk looked and felt while Kristina was gone.

One day while expecting a phone call from Kristina, LaMonica received a surprised phone call from Angie instead. She had called periodically throughout LaMonica's childhood since elementary. Usually Mama would get on the second phone and listen in while she spoke with her. Mama often warned, "Don't tell Angie what school you attend!"

She had asked too.

"Mama, why can't I tell Angie what school I go too?" LaMonica had asked back in elementary school.

"Because I said so," Mama had shot back. "And because it's not safe."

Now that LaMonica was a teenager, Mama allowed her to talk with Angie directly on the phone alone. The calls were sporadic. Sometimes she would go years without calling, then she would pick up and begin calling frequently. Many times the calls were collect because Angie was calling out of Detroit. Mama would accept them but then limit LaMonica on how long she could talk.

Angie would update LaMonica on where she was and what she had been up to. Once she called from a mental facility. She also would ask LaMonica what her favorite songs were and share hers as well. She didn't know where her sister Ambrosia was. Her last boyfriend had taken her from her, and she had been searching ever since.

On this phone call, Angie dropped a bombshell. She was in the hospital.

"I just had you a baby brother. His name is Jackie Thomas McAllen." Jackie for her favorite Jackson five member, and Thomas for her favorite basketball player.

"Oh, my goodness. I can't wait to see him," LaMonica was so excited.

A day or two later Angie called to say that "they" had taken LaMonica's little brother away.

"They took Jackie away from me, LaMonica."

"Who took Jackie and why?"

"The hospital and the State of Michigan. They said he's going to an orphanage until he gets adopted, but I can visit him."

All kinds of thoughts were running through LaMonica's head. She didn't want her little brother out there lost somewhere in Detroit with other people. If they weren't going to let Angie have him, then she wanted him there with her. She hung up with Angie and filled Mama in on what was going on.

"They took my little brother, Mama. I want him. Can you adopt him so I can take care of him?" LaMonica knew Mama used to be a foster parent and a licensed child care provider. She was in good standing with the State of Michigan. She could get this done.

"No, I can't take care of no baby, LaMonica."

"Please Mama, you wouldn't have to do anything. I would do all the work. I just need you to get him for me."

"LaMonica, you have to go to school, you won't be here to take care of a child. Now my answer is no and that's the end of it."

LaMonica was sorely disappointed. She didn't ask Mama anymore, but she didn't give it up either. One day she would get her little brother.

Angie's calls stopped again, and LaMonica could only hope for the best.

KRISTINA STAYED GONE for months and months. The police finally found her when her older boyfriend had to tow a car that was involved in an accident. They recognized Kristina from their runaway list and took her to a runaway shelter, and finally she was reunited with Mrs. Belk.

While Kristina was on the lam LaMonica became close with a new friend. Her name was Lynn. Lynn had recently moved into the Heritage High School district, but she had grown up all her life on the east side. LaMonica and Lynn were one of the few Black girls that had been raised in the hood but attended Heritage High School. Culturally, they were very much the same. Heritage was predominantly White, and the Black teens who attended the school mostly all grew up with the other students there in that neighborhood. They were all pretty nice for the most part, but they simply couldn't relate to LaMonica and Lynn the way they could relate to each other.

LaMonica and Lynn brought all the flava to Heritage High School, and the White kids loved it. They were the jokesters in the classrooms. The ones that were quick to take the White kids' dares and carry them out. This landed them often in detention for not following the rules of the school.

This was fine for Lynn because she lived in the Heritage High School district. For LaMonica, however, it was not.

After multiple antics, LaMonica and Lynn both got

suspended. This caused the school to look further into LaMonica's residency. They checked with the apartment that Mrs. Powers listed as her home address in the school district, and they found that she did not have a lease at that apartment.

18

CULTURE SHOCK

M rs. Powers had not enrolled LaMonica into open enrollment that year because she had missed the cutoff date on account of LaMonica attending Heritage High School with a faulty address. Once the school found out that LaMonica lived outside of the school district they informed Mrs. Powers that she could either pay out of district tuition or she would have to leave the school and go to her own district. The tuition was an exorbitant amount, so Mrs. Powers had no choice but to remove LaMonica from Heritage High School.

She tried to enroll LaMonica in each of the high schools in Saginaw, but because of the missing half a credit, they would not accept her. She then tried to place her back in South Junior High School, but because she had missed the open enrollment cutoff date, she could not attend there either.

For the first time in her life, she had to attend a school in her own neighborhood. She had to attend Central Junior High School. LaMonica had never attended an all-Black school before in her life. This was going to be interesting.

As soon as LaMonica hit the doors of Central Junior High, she met a cousin on her father's side (one of the more well to do, Lincolns) named Carla. From being around her brothers so much LaMonica had a very weird walk for a girl. She had what they called a pimp walk.

"Oh, I know you can fight. You walk like you can fight," Carla said.

Little did Carla know nothing was further from the truth. LaMonica had just turned into a tomboy from hanging around mostly boys (her brothers and cousins) all the time. Even though Mama was rough and tough she had taught LaMonica to be the very opposite.

Initially, she tried to make the best of it and focus on her strengths. LaMonica found out right away that she did well in English class and Spanish class. The Spanish teacher was very impressed with the way LaMonica could roll her r's and the level of Spanish that she knew already.

English, reading and writing had always been important to LaMonica. The English teacher (Ms. Jankowski) she had at Central was very passionate about writing. This motivated her. Often LaMonica would write thought-provoking papers on controversial topics she saw going on in the hood and at that school. When she would turn them in to Ms. Jankowski, she would be so impressed that she would read them aloud to the students, never revealing who the writer was for LaMonica's safety.

The essays touched on topics such as drugs in the school and other ailments of the Black community that they could overcome. One sensitive topic that LaMonica covered was girl on girl violence in the school over boys. This had become LaMonica's most pressing issue since attending Central Junior High.

The tone was set from day one on that first lunch hour.

LaMonica was pretty, with natural long hair that she had professionally styled every two weeks. The boys went crazy over her. Mama had reached retirement age and had started receiving Social Security in addition to her employment income. Also, because LaMonica was Mama's dependent, she received a small monthly check from Social Security.

Now there seemed to be no limits to the fashion LaMonica could buy. And she had all the name brand clothes. She had the blue and white Jordans when they first came out. She had Guess jeans, Karl Kani, Skidz, the latest Nike jogging suits, Nike Cortez, Team dusters (long coats with team names on them). All the name brands from the 90s. LaMonica was fine (the hood term for beautiful) and what they called "fresh da def" in those days.

On that first lunch hour, a boy in the school tried to holler at her by giving her his phone number. LaMonica had no idea what hood protocol was for these situations because (other than Juan) she had only interacted with boys from west side or suburban schools at that point. But she was about to learn a tough lesson.

His "girlfriend" who LaMonica didn't even know existed, found her during the lunch hour.

"You was talkin' to my man?" Keisha asked with strong Ebonics.

Keisha was obviously very popular because she had a team of girls with her when she asked LaMonica this question.

"Yeah uh huh we heard you was talkin' to her man," they all chimed in aggressively.

Once LaMonica determined who they were talking about she answered their questions with no problem.

"He gave me his number, and I wasn't planning to call

him, anyway. Now that I know he's your boyfriend, I definitely won't. Okay!"

Honestly, LaMonica didn't see anything spectacular about this dude, anyway. She wasn't impressed, and certainly she didn't want to argue over him. She hoped the matter was over as the girls walked away, but saw that they all still carried an attitude.

As those first days passed by at Central Junior High, LaMonica saw more and more of the climate at that school. The girls' conversations seemed to revolve around boys, which wasn't unusual. But what was unusual was how often they talked about fighting other girls over boys.

Girls regularly had plans to fight other girls and stories of how they had been either scarred by razor blades or scarred others in fights. LaMonica would often be walking down the halls and girls would just break out into swinging and fighting each other, beating each other like they were in a wild kingdom. She definitely wanted no part of that.

Mama had a few sayings at home about dating the Black male population. According to her, "Niggas ain't bleep." She would often say, "LaMonica watch out for these niggas. I'm tellin' you I could write a book about these niggas."

Deep within her, LaMonica wanted to motivate the other students from solving all their problems by fighting about everything (especially these boys) which seemed to be their main priority. The best way she knew of how to convey information was through her writing. This inspired her to write another essay about it and turn it into the English teacher.

The fighting was so prevalent at Central that Ms. Jankowski was grateful there was a student who had a different perspective on ownership of men and fighting for "their property rights." She read it right away. There was a huge reaction from the class.

A lot of the students weren't open to receive this information and you could hear it in their tone of voice.

"Who wrote that?" One student said after hearing it.

"Yeah who wrote that?" Others began to inquire.

"Don't worry about who the author is. Just know this is something thought-provoking for you to listen to and consider," Ms. Jankowski said.

After the first run in with Keisha, daily lunch hour continued to be problematic for LaMonica. As she would enter the cafeteria, there was always some boy giving her compliments or trying to holler at her. LaMonica knew it was best to ignore them, so she did. But this didn't stop the other girls from getting upset at her for what their "supposed" boyfriends were doing.

Keisha's boyfriend tried to holler at her the hardest, even though he knew this upset Keisha greatly. She began telling her friends she was going to fight LaMonica within the week. Some of her friends passed the information along and it got back to LaMonica.

Mama had always taught her that because of her heart surgery it would not be wise for her to engage in a physical fight so LaMonica never wanted to fight with anyone. After hearing the rumors that this girl wanted to fight her, LaMonica brought weapons to school just in case. This place was like a jungle, and she needed the proper tools to survive in it. LaMonica felt like she had literally stepped inside the movie Lean On Me.

She mentioned to some of the girls that talked to her at school that she was ready with weapons if anybody did anything to her. They secretly passed this information along to the principal. Thank God LaMonica got rid of all that stuff in the middle of the week because the principal conducted a search of her locker. If those weapons would have been found she would have been locked up in Juvenile for at least a year.

LaMonica could tell tensions were getting high at school because a lot of the girls were rolling their eyes at her in the halls and Keisha was clearly upset that her boyfriend wouldn't give up his infatuation with her.

One day after lunch hour, Keisha decided that she had had enough of her boyfriend trying to get with LaMonica. One would think that her "having enough" would entail her breaking up with him for someone who treated her with respect. But oh no, apparently that wasn't the hood relationship way. Keisha decided it was time to fight LaMonica.

When the bell rang after lunch hour as LaMonica was walking up the stairs lo-and-behold Keisha was at the top of the stairs waiting on her along with a gang of girls. They were all rowdy and ready to see a fight. Thank goodness a school hall person happened to make it there and interfered before anything drastic could happen.

LaMonica and Keisha were both taken to the principal's office. This very situation is most likely what developed LaMonica's defense mechanism of resulting to arrogance and condescending when being backed into a corner, feeling hurt, or threatened.

"Don't try to fight me at school because when I come to school, I come here to get my education. I don't come here to fight over a boy."

Keisha was certainly surprised at that reaction from LaMonica. It wasn't what she was used to from other girls.

LaMonica directed her attention to the principal.

"I don't understand what is wrong with your students principal. When I went to Heritage or South Junior High

School, nothing like this ever happened. Can you please get your students in order? How are you allowing them to act like this?" LaMonica spoke to the principal boldly and with a condescending tone. She wanted to make it known she was not a ghetto ignorant person who needed to fight over boys or needed to fight at school.

The principal shot her a few words back. "And why are you here at this school?"

"Because this is my district school and I have to complete a half a semester before going to high school."

"Yes, but didn't Heritage kick you out?"

"Yes, after they found out I didn't live in that district."

"So what I have on my hands is a student who was kicked out of a school in the suburbs, just after count day. They got all the money for you and then sent you over here."

He proceeded to address LaMonica's other concern by making excuses. He called it a culture change. He said he understood that LaMonica was going through a culture change. And she needed to learn how things worked at a Black school.

"Things are just different here. At a White school if you say, 'yo' mama' the kids may just say something mean back and laugh. But at a Black school you need to understand that if you say, 'yo' mama' those are fighting words and a fight is going to happen."

LaMonica could not believe this ridiculousness that she was hearing. She decided that obviously she couldn't be at this school with these people who acted like street boxers while the principal co-signed it.

LaMonica's brother Chuck also attended the school. He had tried to stay out of the situation because it involved girls. But he had heard Keisha was not willing to give this up, and that LaMonica was potentially going to be jumped by her and her friends at the next lunch hour, even after the meeting in the principal's office. The following day he walked her to the cafeteria to make sure no girls jumped on her. As soon as he and LaMonica entered the lunch room Keisha, her cousins and all her friends were standing there waiting on LaMonica. Keisha's cousin, Asia, spoke up.

"Ain't no boy finna fight my cousin," she said

"Well, all of y'all girls ain't fixing to jump on my sister either," Chuck responded.

The girls backed off. But this presented another problem. Now these girls might feel compelled to get their male family members involved. Chuck's mother Birdie called LaMonica at home.

"See, this is why I didn't want you and Chuck going to the same school. I don't want him getting into fights or suspended trying to protect you, LaMonica."

LaMonica felt so stuck. There was no help from anywhere, certainly not from the principal. And she didn't want to cause Chuck problems, so she did the only thing she knew to do, skip school. LaMonica only had a short time to be at Central Junior High before she would receive the credit she needed to transfer to high school. She couldn't wait until the half a semester was up and they moved her forward. She continued to turn in her assignments but found various friends who lived near Central that were either expelled or suspended that she could chill with. She was just biding her time.

19

THE BISHOP MAKES HIS MOVE

In the meantime, the fair came to Saginaw as it does yearly. Every year Mama had a booth in the barns she ran for the Police Community Relations Commission (PCRC). She would help drum up interest for the group and encourage others to start neighborhood associations while passing out Crime Stopper flyers. LaMonica usually helped Mama man the booth, but now that she was older Mama agreed to let LaMonica leave her side and walk around the fair and enjoy the rides on her own.

Saginaw didn't have many events, so many of the teenagers looked forward to the fair every year. It was a great place for the opposite sex to give and get phone numbers. But LaMonica had already decided if anyone approached her, she wasn't giving them the time of day. She had become very guarded when it came to talking to boys now. After she saw how crazy hood chicks could be about dudes. It was like they turned into feral cats.

LaMonica noticed that Black dudes from the hood didn't take rejection well. They would often get angry if a girl wasn't interested in them. Well, these crazy females had turned her into a snob when it came to boys and they would just have to accept that. If they wanted someone to blame for their rejection, they could lay the blame on them, because she didn't want any of these males coming up to her trying to holler.

The fair was located on Webber Street on the east side, and people from all races attended. Often fights would break out when someone from two different gangs would spot each other. The police were in high attendance, so things rarely escalated past a quick scuffle. The police would escort them out of the park and that would be the end of that.

While walking around LaMonica saw all sorts of teenagers dressed in their best outfits and having fun. All the pretty girls had their hair professionally done. The Black girls had their hair beautifully pressed out and the Mexican girls with long hair had wavy crimps.

LaMonica spotted some of her Mexican friends and played games with them. They walked around eating good fair food like vinegar with fries, corn dogs, and elephant ears. And they enjoyed the rides together. She had an all-around good time.

Of course, the boys did start to notice her and began asking for her phone number. She quickly became snobby with each and every one of them, cutting them off and removing herself from their gaze.

Then out of nowhere LaMonica saw Bishop, Lisa's godbrother. She decided she wouldn't be that way with him because he was Lisa's godbrother and she had met him before. He didn't seem like the type to have a bunch of girl-friends, so she gave him the time of day. They walked and talked and she gave him her phone number. LaMonica told Bishop that Mama was very strict. She would have to talk to her first to see if she could get phone calls and visits from a boy now that she was close to being sixteen.

Bishop spoke to Mama on the phone and asked for permission to come visit. Surprisingly, not only did Mama agree he could start calling, but she wanted to meet him and agreed that he could come over to the house and visit strictly on the interior porch.

On the day Bishop was scheduled to come over, LaMonica was waiting for him with anticipation. Never had she had a boy like her who owned a car before. He seemed so much more of an adult than the regular boys her age. He pulled up in Mama's driveway in a raggedy Chevette.

LaMonica didn't notice it was raggedy, she was just happy a boy with a car was coming over to visit her. But the condition of his car was the first thing Mama noticed. She had a scowl on her face. "Look at that raggedy car, LaMonica. Is this the nigga you wanted to come over and visit?"

LaMonica just let that question hang in the air like it was rhetorical.

Bishop came over and met Mama. She wasn't too impressed with him. But she allowed him to stay and visit on the inside porch. The interior porch had windows that were right next to Mama's room so she could go back and forth and monitor what was going on the whole time, although she did allow LaMonica time for *some* privacy up to a point.

Bishop had tried to make a good impression on Mrs. Powers by formerly introducing himself, shaking her hand and having small talk, but it was to no avail. The more he talked, the less she liked him. Bishop let out that he worked on cars with the neighbor who lived two houses away from Mama, Carter. Carter housed a lot of drug users, including himself. Between the loud music, the fights and the junky car parts in his yard, Carter's house was often a source of irritation for Mama. Carter had been a mentor to Bishop ever since he had begun living on his own (with his brother) at the age of thirteen. He taught him how to work on his car and how to survive on his own without a parent. Yes, Bishop had been driving a car since he was thirteen. Bishop had been responsible to do a lot of adult things ever since he was a child.

LaMonica's heart went out to him because of the unfair life he had lived, but it immediately became clear that she and Bishop didn't have very much in common through their conversation. He had been raising himself since he was a thirteen-year-old boy along with his older brother. Now at eighteen he had the conversation of someone much older who held adult responsibilities.

LaMonica's mindset was still that of a teenager at fifteen years old. The most important things to her were if Mama was gonna kick in some extra money to help her finally get a fat gold chain to match her Mickey Mouse gold spinner ring? Would Mama take her down to Flint on the weekend to find an outfit that no one else had so she could rock it to the next Saginaw High Football game - where this whole fashion ensemble would be appreciated?

Bishop's conversation consisted of striving to live. Where was he going to get his next roll of toilet paper from? How it was unfair they had cut his water off and ways he devised to get the money to pay for it. He offered to ask Mama if he could take her out on a date (at his house) and make her something to eat once his water was connected again and he got his food stamps. LaMonica and Bishop were definitely not speaking the same language.

LaMonica didn't mind him coming over to visit because (at Mama's house) she was an only child and she was often bored. Having someone new come over was exciting and helped pass away the time, but she didn't feel any sort of chemistry connection with him, nor much attraction. What she felt was charity. LaMonica had always wanted to be a social worker to help people like him in the world. If she could figure out a way to help him, she would.

Bishop left after visiting for about an hour. And as soon as he left, Mama promptly came out to the interior porch and let LaMonica know that he was some trash. He drove an old beat-up car; he dressed in old clothes and he smelled funny.

"Can't you smell that smell out here on the porch? LaMonica that boy is some trash."

LaMonica hadn't noticed until Mama pointed it out. She guessed it was from him doing the best he could, not having any water in the house. As LaMonica had gotten older she had become more outspoken with her opinions with Mama. And Mama and LaMonica's opinions always differed when it came to the people in the neighborhood in general. Mama found the drug dealers and users to be a source of irritation and a blight on the community, especially since it affected her property values and quality of life. LaMonica understood that part, but she also looked deeper at the factors that had placed them there. This is why she wanted to be a social worker one day.

Bishop had really messed up when he mentioned his relationship with the neighbor Carter. That sealed his fate. Mama went on to say she didn't trust him because Carter was also known as a thief and a drug addict and she didn't want Bishop back over to her house.

"Besides LaMonica you still ain't old enough to be courtin' yet, you're only fifteen not sixteen."

Mama agreed to let Bishop continue to call, but that's as far as she would bend. Eventually LaMonica and Bishop's phone calls fizzled out because they just didn't have much in common.

20

CHESTER, CHESTER

The half of a semester at Central Junior High finally ended and LaMonica was promoted to the 10th grade in January. Open enrollment wouldn't start until the fall of the new school year, so LaMonica was being promoted to the east side—majority Black, high school, Saginaw High.

She had some apprehensions about going to Saginaw High given the climate she was met with at Central, who could blame her? She shared her fears with the English teacher, Ms. Jankowski, at Central.

"Man. I can't go to Arthur Hill or Heritage High School, Ms. Jankowski. They're sending me to Saginaw High. The girls probably fight over there too."

Ms. Jankowski tried to calm LaMonica's fears. "I've worked at schools on the east side all my life, and in my experience the girls tend to mature once they reach high school. There is *some* fighting but not nearly the way it is here at Central."

This made LaMonica feel a lot better. Even though she had heard some rough stories about Saginaw High, she decided she would trust Ms. Jankowski. Besides LaMonica's cousin Joy went to school there, so it couldn't be too bad.

LaMonica had gotten to where she didn't want to ride buses to school anymore. The bus was usually filled up to the brim by the time it made it to her stop. She would normally have to stand up and hold on to a rail. Her small frame would sway and fall, trying to remain standing as the bus made its stops and turns. Mama agreed to drive LaMonica to school every day. LaMonica going to Saginaw High was a lot more convenient for Mama because she had patients near the area around the time she needed to be in school. Besides, LaMonica had long ago made it clear she did not want to ride in the car with Ms. Demona **anywhere.**

Mama dropped LaMonica off for her first day of school at the front of Saginaw High. It was early so everyone was standing outside in the winter waiting on the bell to ring. LaMonica was warm enough, though. She had on her black Triple Fat Goose coat.

The bell rang and she made her way down the side of the building near the side entrance doors open to the students. She noticed there were cars there dropping students off. Some of the drivers were young adults and up on the lawn.

A guy that was parked on the lawn in a Jimmy truck called to her.

"Aye, Aye come here for a minute."

LaMonica certainly didn't answer to "aye" so she kept moving, besides hopefully he was talking to someone else.

"Hey you pretty girl with the Triple Fat Goose on. Come here."

In LaMonica's experience, Black dudes didn't take rejection well. They would often call girls the "B" word for refusing to give them attention in the hood. She had gotten lucky at the fair but didn't want to take her chances at ticking this guy off. Most likely his pride would be hurt after calling so much attention to himself on the lawn, so reluctantly she walked up to his truck.

"Dang girl, what's yo' name?"

"LaMonica."

"Well, LaMonica, you're fine as hell! Why haven't I seen you before?"

"I just started going to school here. Today's my first day. I really need to hurry before I'm late."

"Okay, I'm gonna let your fine self go as soon as you give me your phone number."

She didn't know anything about this dude and didn't want to give him her phone number, nor did she want his. Especially after the encounters she had had at Central. But she didn't want to get him upset either.

"My mama doesn't let me get calls from boys."

"Well then, take my number."

"I can't call boys either, sorry."

"Can't you sneak on the phone?"

Oh my gosh dude, just let this go. I'm trying to get out of this and save your pride at the same time, LaMonica thought.

Finally he relented, and LaMonica went inside for her homeroom class.

Everything seemed to be going well, and then LaMonica went into the restroom during lunch hour. Inside were quite a few girls, one of them she knew who lived in the projects, from the programs at First Ward. They called her, Nuggie.

"Hey LaMonica. I need to talk to you," Nuggie said.

Her tone was so serious, *What could Nuggie possibly have to talk to me about?* LaMonica thought.

"I heard my boyfriend was outside trying to talk to you this morning."

"Who's your boyfriend?" LaMonica asked, while thinking, *oh no, not this mess again!*

"They call him, Stacks. He drives a gray Jimmy."

Oh, so that was his name, LaMonica was trying so hard to get away from him that morning she hadn't cared enough to even retain his name.

"Look girl, you can be honest with me. I know my boyfriend has tried to holler at girls before. I'm just checkin' to see if he's still doing it."

"Yeah, he did ask me for my phone number–"

"And what did you say!" Nuggie asked, cutting LaMonica off.

"Girl, I just lied and told him my mother doesn't let me get boy phone calls and he went on."

"Okay. Well thanks for telling me girl."

Nuggie seemed like the situation was over, LaMonica hoped that it was.

In the afternoon LaMonica was off to English class and she was excited about that. Mrs. Peoples from Mt. Olive was the English teacher. LaMonica had often observed her sleeping during church. It was funny because she would wake up on beat right when the choir sang the dismissal song.

Unfortunately, English class turned out to be no different. Mrs. Peoples handed out a school issued basic English book everyone was to read from. She marked the page ranges on the board and promptly retreated to her desk for nap time. Most of the students took a cue from her and did the same thing. LaMonica tried to read the book, but it was just going over basic English rules and boring as ever. This was obviously not challenging enough to keep her attention. How disappointing.

Now that LaMonica was in the 10th grade, she had more

freedom to move around. Her favorite people to be with were her cousin Olivia and her friend Lynn. She still visited Luchie and her family at times, but Luchie now had a baby and was stuck at home most of the time. LaMonica was now enjoying her new found freedom that Mama was beginning to give her.

Mama was still limited on where LaMonica could go but the places and the people that Mrs. Powers approved of - she allotted her a lot of privileged time at those places and with those people. LaMonica spent a great deal of time at her cousin Olivia's grandmother's house (which was also Richard's mother-in-law).

Olivia and LaMonica weren't biological cousins. They had named each other cousins ever since LaMonica's brother Richard had married Olivia's Aunt, Shawna. This was the same wedding that LaMonica had made the vow to pray for and care for the marriage between her brother and her new sister-in-law. LaMonica and Olivia had prayed and took the vow of family unity. Through the lighting of the unity candle 'the Armstrongs' and 'the Powers' family were proclaimed to be one family. Olivia and LaMonica had already been spending time with each other prior to the wedding because of Shawna and Richard's relationship. "We're cousins now," they both happily exclaimed, when the bride and groom kissed.

That was back when they were ten years old. Now that LaMonica was a teenager, she and Olivia still had the same interests and enjoyed each other's company. They were both beautiful girls. Olivia was gorgeous. She was chocolate brown with natural long flowing hair. The boys went crazy over her, just like LaMonica. And just like LaMonica, Olivia was very selective on who she let get close to her.

One day while visiting with Olivia at her grandmother's

house, Olivia's Uncle Chester returned from out of town. Chester had recently moved to Nebraska, where his older brother was employed. He left Saginaw at his mother's request in order to break some of the wrong associations he had fell in with. This wasn't by his choice and so he frequently came back and forth between Omaha, Nebraska and Saginaw, Michigan. Although he spent most of his time in Nebraska now.

Chester was about nineteen or twenty, and very well built. He entertained Olivia and LaMonica with interesting stories about how he danced at clubs with women back in Nebraska. He kept them laughing. Then he began to get flirtatious with LaMonica. Olivia was all for LaMonica and her uncle being boyfriend and girlfriend, but the grandmother had no idea that Chester thought of LaMonica as anything other than family (even though technically they weren't related by blood).

Chester was considered handsome by most girls in his neighborhood. He was chocolate brown like Olivia, had long curly hair and was muscular built. Even though LaMonica was just fifteen he wasn't much taller than her because he was very short in stature.

Chester's flirting became more and more intense with each visit. One night when everyone was asleep in the house, Chester asked her to come down into the basement where his room was located and have a few drinks with him. LaMonica quickly became intoxicated.

She and Chester started kissing. The next thing she experienced, were her clothes coming off, and he had her in the bed. LaMonica had never been naked in a bed with a boy before. She was still a virgin. Things seemed to be moving fast, much faster than she was able to control them. The next thing she knew, Chester was having sex with her.

He didn't handle her like the virgin she was. Everyone in the house had heard them in the basement and knew what happened. This was reported back to Mrs. Powers from the grandmother.

Mama was upset, and this was a weird situation. Her son's brother-in-law who was an adult had had sex with her fifteen-year-old daughter. But being from down south, Mama didn't look at it like statutory rape. Besides, because of Chester's short stature, he looked closer to LaMonica's age.

After the big incident, Chester called LaMonica on the phone and declared to her they were now boyfriend and girlfriend. LaMonica agreed. He would soon be leaving back for Nebraska but told her he would write her frequently and come and see her whenever he was back in town.

In the meantime, Mama believed in finding resources. She found a teen program called Prevention and Youth Services (PAYS). PAYS specialized in preventing pregnancies. They were housed on the other side of Innerlink, which was the runaway shelter LaMonica's friend Kristina had once used.

LaMonica began attending Prevention and Youth Services weekly group meetings. And at Mama's request, they also gave her a special one-on-one sex education class that involved learning how to use condoms. No one could say that Mama didn't do her best to use the resources in her community to help guide her teenage daughter.

In the meantime, when Chester wasn't calling, he was writing LaMonica letters and sending her money. He even sent her a gold chain. He instructed her that she was to remember that she was his girlfriend and she was to wait for him until he came back in town in a few months. LaMonica didn't have much connection with Chester other than that one night that they spent together, but she tried to follow the instructions he gave. She waited months for him to return.

Mama tended to share a lot of things about LaMonica with her friends and family, including Ms. Demona. And you can bet Ms. Demona had lots of opinions about LaMonica's new status as a teenager and a non-virgin.

One day when mama was gone grocery shopping and Ms. Demona was cleaning up the house, she found some records regarding LaMonica in Mama's secret drawer. These were LaMonica's adoption records from the state of Michigan. They broke down everything about LaMonica's family history. It included information about her mother and father and the fact that she had a sister from her mother.

LaMonica was sitting in the living room watching MTV. Ms. Demona exited from Mama's room and walked straight up to the TV that LaMonica was watching and shut it off.

"Oh, so now I know why you half crazy. I just found a report on you in yo' mama's drawer while cleaning it. Do you want to know what it says?" She said with a mocking tone.

LaMonica just looked at her curiously and shocked. She didn't say yes or no, but secretly she kind of wanted to know what it said. She could already see however, that whatever it was, Ms. Demona was going to deliver it harshly.

Ms. Demona repeated herself in a slow, mean tone. "I said - do you - want to know - what this report says?"

"Sure. I guess." LaMonica responded with reluctance.

Ms. Demona began reading from some of the pages in the report:

.   .   .

LAMONICA'S biological mother Angie McAllen was rushed to the hospital during her ninth month of pregnancy for a drug overdose.

Her father Chuck Price worked at the GM Plant but said he had not been the same since he was hit in the head at work. Chuck has several children by several women. He's not financially responsible for most of them and the ones he pays child support for he is often behind in it.

From the time LaMonica was an infant, Angie began leaving her in an unrelated home with Ella Mae Powers. She later moved to Detroit and had another child, LaMonica's sibling, Ambrosia Copeland. Eventually she left Ambrosia in an unrelated home and she is currently being raised in the city of Detroit in a home unregulated by the State of Michigan. It is unclear if Chuck Price is the father of both children.

THE REPORT APPEARED to be several pages, but Ms. Demona just read from some of it. Even though LaMonica had heard most of these things before it upset her to know they were in an official report. Now it was verified that they were real and true. The way Ms. Demona was delivering this news was super nasty and super harsh.

"I'm surprised they ain't got nothing in here about yo' mama being a whore. I knew it was a matter of time until you would turn into a whore just like her. You done finally got caught sleepin' with a boy. I tell you LaMonica, you ain't no good. You ain't no earthly good. Uh, uh uh."

Ms. Demona went back into Mama's room and put the papers back in the drawer. Then she went in the kitchen and grabbed some clothes that were in the dryer to take upstairs to fold. She took one look at LaMonica, shook her head and turned her nose up at her while she walked down the hall.

On her way up the stairs all the while she was saying, "uh, uh, uh."

So many bad feelings were running through LaMonica right then and there. Everything that Ms. Demona was trying to accomplish was working. She was trying to make LaMonica feel less than zero, and it had worked. LaMonica was beyond upset. She went in her room and grabbed some quarters for the payphone and with tears streaming down her face she ran out of the front door of the house. LaMonica ran around the corner to Augie's Superette store to use their outside payphone.

In Chester's last letter, he said he would be back in town soon. She wondered if he had made it, and maybe he could come pick her up. LaMonica frantically dialed Chester's number at his mother's house in town. She wanted someone to hurry and pick her up before Mama or Ms. Demona found out where she was. At this point no one had come looking for her yet, and she had to hurry. LaMonica decided she did not want to be around either of them or in that house anymore with the way she was being treated and made to feel.

Chester's mother answered. He wasn't in town and he wouldn't be there for probably another week.

LaMonica was trying to think of who else had a car or who she could get a hold of that could get access to one. Sometimes her friend Lynn would sneak her mother's car out of the driveway when she could. She tried calling Lynn, but there was no answer. LaMonica was so frantic at this point. She had to get away from off of 6th Street at the store payphone before Mama or Ms. Demona found her.

21

RUNAWAY CHILD

Suddenly Bishop pulled up in his Chevette. He parked his car in the middle of the one-way street, got out and said, "Hey what are you doing? What you up to?"

"I gotta get out of here. I'm trying to call somebody to pick me up."

"Well, you need a ride?"

LaMonica responded, "Yes!"

LaMonica hopped into Bishop's car and he asked, "Where are you going?"

"I'm just trying to hurry up and leave before my mama finds me," LaMonica really had no clear destination.

Bishop took LaMonica around the corner to his house on Norman Street. She told him she was hiding from Mama and she didn't want to go home.

"You can stay here with me," he said.

Bishop told her that his brother was currently in prison up north. And he was the only one there. She was welcomed to stay with him.

When LaMonica and Bishop made it to his house, he

was super excited that she was there. He seemed to have boundless energy. He jumped up and down when he talked and was very animated.

"Yo' check this out. I been to jail twice since I last seen you. Yeah, and right before that I had to fight a couple of niggas. One had a knife, and I had to hold the blade while swinging and fighting him, like this here." Bishop began acting out everything he was explaining to her.

Bishop went on to share the things that were important to him with LaMonica. He talked about more of the fights he'd been in and the crimes he had committed. This gangster side of Bishop intrigued LaMonica, because she and her friends were all beginning to be attracted to bad boys. The gangster thug life was very much the trend.

"What gang are you in?" LaMonica asked.

"Oh nawl. I ain't in no gang. Me and my brother prefer to do our work alone. Gangs is for suckas. They take orders. I don't take orders from nobody.

"Being in a gang reminds me of taking orders, and taking orders reminds me of slavery. You know there's still slavery going on, right? Yep, right up there up north where my brother is locked up at. My brother is a slave in that prison, boot camp. When I go up there, they're making him say yes sir and no sir. Telling him when he can turn the lights on and off and when he can go to bed. My brother writes me and tells me, them honkys talkin' down to him all day like a slave."

"When will he be out?" LaMonica asked.

"Oh, he's coming home soon. I can't wait to be the one to pick him up either. I'm gonna talk to them honkys like they're my hoes when I do."

Later LaMonica would find out that Bishop's brother Alonzo was locked up for robbing and beating an elderly woman. He clearly was not a nice guy. But according to Bishop, his brother was being treated unjustly, and this was slavery.

Bishop's excitement easily influenced LaMonica. Over the next few days, he shared all sorts of things with her. Even intimate details of his life. He encouraged her to finish school because he had cried tremendously when he didn't graduate and his high school class came celebrating and beeping their horns down his street. Bishop didn't graduate from high school because he had very little support and had to live on his own.

Then he told her the whole awful tale of how he had come to raise himself from thirteen and up and why it came to be. The awful tale is his and his only to share, and so perhaps one day he will with others. But LaMonica regarded all that Bishop said to her in her heart. She was beginning to care for him after he had shown such vulnerabilities.

Even though Bishop was now an adult, he couldn't let go of the hurt feelings from all those years he had to fend for himself as a child. He felt very slighted in life. And LaMonica understood him. For different reasons, she felt the same way.

"My great aunt bought this house for me and my brother, and I've been taking care of myself ever since."

"Dang B, that's messed up," LaMonica said.

"I've just been out here living like this, trying to survive. Growing up, if me and my brother needed toilet paper, we had to steal it. We didn't have nothin'."

Bishop said he still had to steal all of his essentials except for food. Now that he was over eighteen, he received food stamps every month. Bishop was on welfare. He received a check from the State of Michigan from a program that was called General Assistance. It offered free benefits to help men and women who didn't have children and didn't work. The monthly amount was minimal about $160.

"Yeah, they give women with children more than double that," he had remarked while looking at LaMonica for a reaction.

Bishop was very braggadocios about his ability to demand his welfare benefits from "the honkys." He said he liked to wear his worst clothes and go up to the welfare building, demanding that they hurry up and get his money and his food stamps together whenever something had delayed them.

Everything that Bishop talked about went completely opposite to the values that Mama had taught LaMonica. Mama had taught LaMonica to work for a living and that using the system is not right. Mama often had conversations with LaMonica warning her not to turn out like the people of the neighborhood.

As more and more renters moved into Mama and LaMonica's neighborhood, there began to be lots of women who used the welfare system. Mama would often say, "LaMonica don't ever become like these foolish women who rent houses with their welfare checks and then have a bunch of kids with a no count man laying up on them. These foolish women are sitting up here taking care of a man."

LaMonica had mostly just listened to Bishop. He was older and had a much stronger personality than hers. His way of thinking was new to her.

He asked her why she wanted to get away from home. LaMonica didn't know how to put everything that was going on at home into words, so she just said, "My mama doesn't let me do nothin'."

Bishop responded, "Yeah I know your mama's strict on

you but that's what I first liked about you. That way I knew you would be at home and not running the streets. That's why I want you to be my girl."

BISHOP DIDN'T LIKE to sit up in the house for long. He was used to running the streets. So as the days passed by, he and LaMonica hit the streets in his Chevette. Even though he was just eighteen years old, buying alcohol was no problem for him. He often frequented the liquor stores on the east side. He had no driver's license because of multiple tickets, and the license plate that was on his car wasn't even his. He bragged about how he had stolen it from another car.

Bishop liked to drink while he drove. He would ride all over the east side on the back streets, real slow, to avoid the police, always holding a 40 ounce of beer or malt liquor between his legs. When the alcohol would run out, he would make another stop at the liquor store.

Blasting his music loudly was important to him too. As he and LaMonica rode around the back streets of the hood, they listened to rap music. A lot of it demeaned women. Whenever a lyric would come on that called women the "B" word, he would turn it down and say, "I'm gonna turn that down because I don't want you to think that I look at you that way."

Bishop and LaMonica were riding during the time of day that she normally would've been at school. She felt free. Free from Mama's overprotection and free from Ms. Demona's harsh treatment and words.

Bishop stopped them at the Howard Street Market liquor store. The liquor store was right across the street from the teen center, Innerlink/PAYS where LaMonica had weekly meetings at. She told Bishop this, so he moved the car to the side of the liquor store so she wouldn't be seen.

"I'm going in here to get me a 40 ounce. What do you want to drink?"

"I don't know," LaMonica responded.

"Don't worry, I got just the right thing for you," Bishop told her.

Bishop returned to the car with a 40 ounce of Big Bear malt liquor and a 2 liter bottle of Sun Country wine cooler.

"Here, sip on this while we ride."

Bishop passed her a red Solo cup and a bag of chips while he poured her some of the wine cooler.

"I would have got me an Old English 800, that's my favorite, but I wanted to make sure I could get you something you would like."

Old English 800 was $3, and the off brand, Big Bear was only $1. Bishop hoped LaMonica appreciated the sacrifices he was making for her.

They rode around all day like this with Bishop throwing up his hand and blowing his horn at lots of people in the hood and exchanging hood greetings with them. He seemed to know a lot of people in the ghetto, especially people older than him. He was popular in general with people walking to liquor stores or who appeared to be walking while selling or using drugs.

While they were out riding LaMonica had called Mama on the payphone to let her know she was okay. She remembered how worried Kristina's mother had been when she was missing, and she didn't want to put Mama through that. As soon as Mama would start asking detailed questions about where she was and who she was with, she'd hang up the phone.

22

THE PLAN

Bishop and LaMonica rode around like this over the next few days. Then he introduced a proposition to her. He had shared his soul with her. How his family life was and the things that made him cry. He even had let her sleep next to him night after night, which was a huge privilege he felt he had extended to her. His belief was you always have to watch your back, no matter who it was. And he had trusted LaMonica not to rob him and everything. At this point he felt they were bonded.

LaMonica had just listened. Knowing all of his struggles gave her a heart for him. At one point Bishop said to her, "Tell me about *your* problems. I know you have problems too. Share them with me."

LaMonica found it hard to share with him because the issues she was facing didn't seem to compare to his, but they were insurmountable to her. Also, she didn't have the language at fifteen to say, "I'm being emotionally abused and possibly physically abused at home and I feel jailed and caged in." She didn't know how to put that into words, so she just told him she didn't want to live with her mama anymore.

"I just need to get away from there," LaMonica explained.

"Okay, well peep this. You can move in here with me and we can have a baby. Then you can get a welfare check every month for money."

LaMonica thought about it, but she wasn't sure. Bishop kept bringing it up day after day, though. She had to admit it had been very freeing riding around the city with him. She had been able to breathe the last few days without people saying harsh, mean things to her. Even riding around with Bishop every day, drinking and doing his favorite things felt better than being at home with Mama. It wasn't the type of thing she and the friends her age would normally choose as fun, but it beat being at home in her situation. The thought of living at Mama's house again felt scary. Now that she had runaway, she had passed the point of no return. Things were sure to get worse when she returned home.

She finally gave in and told Bishop they could try to have a baby. They made love in ways they thought would purposely help LaMonica get pregnant. Once, when they were in the middle of the throes of passion, there was a knock on the door. Bishop was always cautious about who was at the door because he never knew if it was an enemy or the police. He was constantly committing crimes against other people, and he fully expected for that to come back on him at any given moment. Besides that, he never knew if a warrant had been issued for him for the latest thing he had done. While LaMonica was there, he was constantly standing at the sides of the windows and peeping out of them.

Bishop looked out of a slit in one of the curtains in the

windows and ascertained that it was Mrs. Powers knocking at the front door.

He ran into the bedroom, "It's yo' mama."

Just as he said that you could hear Mama talking as she tapped on the door harder and harder, "Hello is anybody home? Hello."

With anxiety LaMonica exclaimed, "Don't answer it!"

"I have to answer it. She sees my car outside. If I don't answer it, it'll look suspicious."

Bishop was criminal minded, so he knew how these things worked. He had often schemed and scammed people, and he had experience in making it appear that he was on the up and up with things. LaMonica was naïve to all of this. She stayed hidden in the bedroom while Bishop opened the door.

"Bishop, have you seen my daughter?" Mrs. Powers asked.

"No, Mrs. Powers, I haven't seen LaMonica in a long time. I think the last time I saw her was when I visited on yo' porch way back." Bishop said this while he nervously stroked his beard.

"Oh okay, because she's been missing now for about five days. I thought maybe you had heard from her, so I got your address from Carter."

"No, I haven't heard from her Mrs. Powers. Besides, I don't have a phone anymore. I hope she's okay. If I see her out anywhere, I'll make sure to get a hold of you."

Bishop came back in and closed the door. "Your mama seems worried. But at least I made sure she won't be calling the police over here."

Since Bishop didn't have a phone LaMonica decided as soon as she was near one she would check in with Mama again.

Bishop and LaMonica got dressed, and they began going riding for the day. Bishop was proud of his new beautiful girlfriend, so he took her to meet his family. First, they went by his aunt and uncle's home. Then they visited his mother's house. They were all very surprised to see such a pretty girl with Bishop, but they were happy about it.

While LaMonica was at Bishop's mother's house she used the phone in the kitchen to call and tell Mama again that she was okay.

Mama was really upset this time. "It's been six days, LaMonica when are you coming home?" Mama angrily asked.

"And where are you, anyway?"

"Mama, I just called to let you know I'm okay." It was hard for LaMonica to resist answering Mama's questions, and she might answer the wrong one and give away too many clues, so she couldn't stay on the phone long with her.

LaMonica also called to check in with her friend Lynn.

"Oh my goodness girl, I've been worried about you. Where have you been?"

LaMonica spoke freely with Lynn and told her she had been with Bishop at his house. Lynn's mother had been listening to their conversation in the house.

"Lynn-Marie, if you know where that girl is, you'd better tell Mrs. Powers. If something bad happens to her while she's out there in them streets that will be on your conscious forever."

Lynn didn't follow her mother's advice right away. But then Mrs. Powers began calling and calling and stopping by.

"Lynn, tell Mrs. Powers where LaMonica is before she gets hurt out there."

"She's with that boy Bishop Mrs. Powers," Lynn admitted.

Mrs. Powers went back to Bishop's house, but his car was gone. She waited a lengthy time and there was no return.

After having dinner at Bishop's mother's house, she offered for LaMonica and Bishop to spend the night. LaMonica and Bishop spent the night at his mother's house, and they returned back to his house on Norman Street in the morning.

As soon as they were settled inside the house Mama was at the door. This time she wasn't knocking gently, she was banging on the door.

"Open this door! I know you have my daughter in there. Open this door now!"

Bishop and LaMonica knew better than to answer the door this time. Mrs. Powers became so angry because she knew LaMonica was inside that house she took a rock and bust out Bishop's big bay living room window. Then she screeched off in the car.

Within about 15 minutes, the police were at Bishop's door and he had no choice but to open up and release LaMonica to them.

Mrs. Powers was outside on the sidewalk waiting for him to bring LaMonica out of the house. The police told Mrs. Powers that she had to stand back and let them talk to LaMonica and Bishop alone for a minute. Bishop told the police officers that Mrs. Powers had busted his windows out. But Because Mrs. Powers was a member of the Police Community Relations Commission (PCRC) she was friends with all the police. As a matter of fact, she often had lunch with some of the sergeants. That's why they had made it there so fast.

"Come and look and see what this woman did to my window!" Bishop urged the police.

"Listen Bishop, we all know Mrs. Powers really well. She

wouldn't do anything like that. Looks like you broke that window from the inside yourself, son."

The police questioned LaMonica and asked her did she want to go home or would she rather go to the runaway center, Innerlink.

"I want to go to Innerlink," LaMonica responded.

Mama was shocked. *Why would LaMonica prefer to go to a shelter instead of coming home?* "I want her to come home with me right now," Mrs. Powers demanded.

"I'm sorry, Mrs. Powers. It's just a formality. If a teen declares they choose to go to the runaway shelter, we're obligated to take them. But honestly, they can't sign themselves in anyway. She'll need your permission to stay once she gets there. You can follow us in the car if you'd like," the officer responded.

When LaMonica arrived at the Innerlink runaway shelter, they took her into a room with a counselor. She told the counselor she wanted to stay. That's when the counselor informed her that the rule at the shelter was that a minor had to have a parent sign a consent form to stay.

Mama pulled up and was escorted into the counseling office with LaMonica and the counselor. The counselor had all the paperwork ready for Mama to sign.

"I'm not signing this! LaMonica needs to come home. I will not agree to this at all," Mrs. Powers stated.

"Well, she's saying that she wants to stay. That's actually a good sign, Mrs. Powers. It shows she wants to work on the problems that caused her to run away in the first place. As I've already explained to LaMonica, if you sign her in this won't be a vacation away from home. There's work to be done. She'll have multiple counseling sessions each week. One of those weekly sessions will include working problems out with you. Also, while LaMonica is here, there are visiting days for parents, so you will be able to see your child. And she can call you anytime."

"I don't want that Bishop boy coming up here, seeing her," Mrs. Powers said.

"Oh, absolutely not! Tonight when we fill out paperwork, you will agree to who can and cannot come up to the facility for visits with LaMonica. You also have to sign a permission card for specific people and phone numbers she's able to call. We will dial the numbers for her, and she will only be able to communicate with those you have given consent to. If you choose to only allow her to call your number and have visits with you, then that's all she'll be able to do."

Mama was relieved at hearing this.

"And what about school?"

"We will drive her to and from school. That is the only place she'll be allowed to go outside of the building."

Wait, this is sounding pretty strict, LaMonica thought. But at least she wouldn't have to go home.

After hearing all the rules, Mama finally agreed reluctantly. She'd much rather have LaMonica home with her, but if they could get her to behave before coming home, she was willing to give it a shot.

"She can call me right?"

"Yes, Mrs. Powers, she can call you anytime," the counselor reassured her.

"And we will have visits right?"

"Yes, ma'am."

"And ya'll won't let her go anywhere but school?"

"That's correct."

"Okay. I'll let her stay."

During LaMonica's stay at the Innerlink runaway shelter they drove her to school, picked her back up every day and brought her back to the facility. She was not allowed to leave the facility otherwise, just as the counselor had promised. Bishop tried to send her letters while she was in there, but the letters were intercepted by staff because Mama didn't want him communicating with her at all.

During their counseling appointments, Mama and LaMonica discussed the adoption paperwork that was found at their home. The harsh way it was presented to her wasn't thought of as important to Mama. But she asked her if she would like to see her sister. LaMonica very much wanted to meet her sister, so Mama made a plan to inquire with the State of Michigan on her sister's location. Mama had a lot of pull with the State of Michigan because one of her friends from the Parents Without Partners group worked there. LaMonica knew if Mama really wanted to get something done, she would. So she was excited about finally being able to meet her sister soon.

Other than that issue, LaMonica didn't make a lot of headway in counseling with Mama because she didn't really want to address the issues that made LaMonica not want to be at home.

23

GOOD DEALS GONE BAD

LaMonica had never done well with strict routines. After the newness of Innerlink wore off, the program began feeling way too restrictive. She grew bored, and she rebelled. LaMonica thought it would be cute to use the cuss words she knew in Spanish with the staff. Little did she know those Spanish words were quite popular. They promptly sent her to her bedroom for the entire day after that episode.

This was beginning to feel like another jail cell. She didn't like the fact that they could not leave the building whatsoever. *This is even more of a lockdown than at home,* LaMonica thought. The more restrictions that were placed on LaMonica, the further she would rebel. The more she would rebel, the tougher the restrictions that were being placed on her. First she lost her rec room privileges. Then she was banished to her room for the entire weekend.

Finally, when they were out of punishments they took away her phone call rights. They wouldn't even allow her to call Mama. That's when LaMonica decided she had had enough of Innerlink and she ran away to a house next door.

She found some nice Mexican guys there, and they asked her if she wanted to use the phone. She used the phone, called Mama, and Mama happily came and checked her out of there.

Mama was so happy that LaMonica would rather come home than be at Innerlink that she took her shopping at the mall and bought her some new outfits and name brand shoes to match.

Mama then let her know Bishop had tried to write her letters while she was in Innerlink and the staff had told her about it. That's when LaMonica knew that he still cared. Mama informed her, "I don't want you around that nigga under any circumstances LaMonica."

LaMonica's second hour class at Saginaw High was a rotating requirement class. Every six weeks the class changed over to a new required course. The first six weeks had been Life Skills, which she found enjoyable. The second six weeks was gym class. Once LaMonica returned home from Innerlink her second hour class had switched over.

At first LaMonica thought gym class was going to be cool as long as they didn't push her too hard. Physically, she had limitations that weren't always understood by just looking at her. But the Cardiologist had always told Mama, LaMonica would know her own limits and she should stop then. LaMonica was not able to run and achieve the physical requirements that most teens her age could achieve because her heart worked differently. She would often get winded from too much physical activity.

On the first day of gym class, the teacher explained that everyone was expected to pass several physical challenges and there would be no exceptions. LaMonica didn't want to call attention to herself, but already she could see this was a setup for failure. There was no switching classes either because it was a requirement.

Another graded requirement for gym class was that she change into gym clothes and shower before the end of class in the locker rooms. There was only about 5-10 minutes of time allotted for changing back into your school clothes and showering. LaMonica didn't do well with being rushed. The first time she attended class, this was kind of sprung on her. She had sweated out her professional hair style and had to try to fix it and take a shower all within 10 minutes. This did not work out well. She ended up going to all the rest of her classes, looking crazy for the rest of the day.

Messy hair, half done showers and perhaps even physical activity would have been fine if gym class was later in the afternoon but it was her second hour. So the next day when Bishop just showed up at Saginaw High looking for her, she was overjoyed to jump in the car with him and leave.

This became their daily habit. Mama would drop LaMonica off to school in the morning and Bishop would come and pick her up at second hour so she wouldn't have to go to gym class. They would get so caught up in being together that a lot of the times she didn't even return to school for the rest of her classes. After spending the day with Bishop, he would bring her back to school just before it was time for Mama to come pick her up again.

Because of LaMonica's constant truancy and the fact that she was now sixteen, they placed her on a list of students who were in danger of being dropped from the school. One morning when Bishop hadn't made it to the school to pick her up yet, she heard the list read aloud on the loudspeaker.

The school notified Mama that LaMonica was on this

list, and LaMonica and Mama talked about it during one of their sessions at the counselor's office at Innerlink. She and Mama were still receiving nonresidential services, and they had continued making appointments for counseling as needed.

Mama, LaMonica, and the counselor made a deal that LaMonica could start visiting with Bishop. But he would have to come over to the house for his visits so that Mama could see what they were up to. And if she felt comfortable enough, she would start letting Bishop take her out on dates since she was sixteen at this point.

When Bishop came up to the school, the next morning LaMonica let him know that he could start coming over to visit and she was going to stay at school to keep her agreement with Mama. She then went to the counselor's office and pleaded with them to switch her out of gym class. She even explained about her heart condition. The counselor said without a medical note it could not be done.

With frustration, LaMonica headed to gym class. During this class session the gym teacher began explaining how starting with the following week every student was going to be required to swim in Saginaw High's deep, deep pool. That was it! *There's no way I'm getting in that pool*, LaMonica thought. *I can't even swim and that pool is deep. Nope. Nope. Nope.* LaMonica decided she would go to every other class (even the sleeping English class) but not this one. Hopefully, with her just missing one class per day, it wouldn't be too noticeable.

Mama kept her agreement and allowed Bishop to come over. She had a quick but serious conversation with him on his first visit.

"Look from what I figure you and LaMonica are having sex now. All I ask is that when y'all have sex, you use rubbers. I don't want my daughter coming up with no baby around here."

"I will, Mrs. Powers," Bishop said.

Bishop agreed to Mama's terms, but secretly he still had plans to have a baby with LaMonica so she could move in with him.

Mama allowed Bishop to come pick LaMonica up for dates. They would often say they were going to see a film or going out to eat, but they never did either of those things unless it was eating at his mama's house. Most of the time they just went back to his house on Norman Street for sex. LaMonica wouldn't have minded going on dates for real, but it wasn't something Bishop could afford.

Mama figured out they weren't really going on dates because she would check up on where they said they had been. If Bishop said he was taking LaMonica to a movie, Mama would inquire on the title of it. She would then go and watch the movie herself so she would know what it was about. Later she would quiz LaMonica on things that occurred in the movie. And of course LaMonica had no clue past what the trailer showed. Sometimes Olivia or one of LaMonica's friends would be over when Mama did this, and they all saw that Bishop wasn't really taking LaMonica anywhere. This unquestionably affected their opinion of him.

Mama began to tell LaMonica things like, "You know that nigga ain't doing nothing but using you, right? Just using you for sex. I don't know why you want to keep going out with some trash like that anyways."

LaMonica listened, and she pressed Bishop to take her on an actual date. He went and scrimped up on some money by cleaning old things up around the house and taking them to Kmart and other retailers for a cash refund.

While LaMonica waited on Bishop to pick her up, she had gotten dressed in one of her nicest Guess Jeans outfits. She had finger waves that waved up high in front and her hair hung down long and silky in the back. She popped in her Nefertiti gold earrings and sprayed on some perfume. For the final touch, she wore her MC Hammer Gazelle glasses. LaMonica stood back and admired herself in the mirror. Now she was ready for her date.

"How do I look, Mama?"

"It doesn't matter how you look because you ain't going out with nothin' but some trash," is all Mama would say.

LaMonica stood at the screen door on the interior porch, waiting on Bishop to pull up in the driveway. He had a lot of conversation for her as soon as she got into the car.

"Check this out, baby, I was tryin' real hard to get us some money. So look here, I took an old fan I had around the house and cleaned it out real good. Then I took it to Kmart and demanded they give me a refund. I was working hard for us, baby. They didn't want to do it, but I argued with the manager until he gave me some money. Then I pawned a few things. Now we've got gas to ride all the way over there and get movie tickets." Again, Bishop hoped LaMonica could see how much he had done to take her on a date.

"Of course we can't buy nothin' once we get there, so you should just stick some snacks in yo' pockets. I'm gonna have some in my shirt."

From the moment they arrived at the movie theater, Bishop seemed agitated. Once they were seated and began watching the movie, Bishop said he felt like Black people were being treated in a racist way in the movie.

"See, this is why I don't go see movies. This will make

me want to hall off and fire on a honky right in his face. This is exactly why I don't go to the movies."

Bishop became so agitated he wanted to leave the movie early. For one, he said the movie was upsetting him and for two; he said he didn't like to ever leave anywhere when everybody else was leaving out. So they didn't get to stay and see the ending.

"Look here baby, this is one them movies niggas like to get to bustin' at. We gotta make a move and get outta here."

LaMonica followed him obediently. When they made it out to the car, they discovered that he had locked his keys in the car. Then they headed back into the movie theater and he inquired with the staff if they had a wire hanger so he could stick it through the window and unlock his car door. Bishop looked rough, and he was still mad at White people from the movie, so he approached them aggressively. The staff took one look at him and had no sympathy for his situation.

"No sorry sir, we no longer hand out wire hangers to people who "say" they've locked their keys in their car because they could be trying to steal an automobile. The best thing we can suggest is that you call the police."

"Man, I don't need no Po Po," Bishop responded.

The movie theater had a coat rack with other people's coats hanging up and wire hangers. Bishop went over and was about to take one.

"Sir. You cannot have a wire hanger from our facility. Now we already advised you to call the police if you've locked your keys in your car. If you keep trying to take property from our business, we will have to call the police ourselves."

LaMonica had just seen her cousin Charlie Jr (Joy's brother) in the halls of the movie theater.

"Bishop my cousin's here and he's a police officer maybe he can help."

"Man F the police and forget these honkys too. Come on, baby let's go," Bishop said.

LaMonica followed behind him in submission.

When they reached the parking lot, Bishop began pulling antennas off of other people's cars. He would try one on the door and it would be too thick, then he would rip another one off until he thought he had found just the perfect size to use on his car window to pull the lock up.

The movies had ended, and people began coming outside to their cars. When they saw what Bishop was doing, they went back in to report it to the movie theater workers.

The manager came outside at this point. "Sir, what is your name?"

"Don't worry about what my name is," Bishop responded.

"Well, we are getting reports that you are out here removing antenna's from people's cars and we can't have that."

Bishop didn't respond right away. But it was clear he had done so because he held a bent up antenna in his hand. The antenna from his own car had long been gone, so he lied and said, "Look here. This is my own antenna from my own car."

"Okay, well, I'm just warning you if we get anymore reports that you are stealing antennas off of people's cars, we will call the police." The manager left and went back inside the building. People in the parking lot were gawking at Bishop in disgust. LaMonica was thoroughly embarrassed, but she didn't dare say it to Bishop.

As soon as the manager was back inside the building, he pulled another antenna off of another car.

"This one looks thin enough. It'll work. We're gonna have to hurry up and get out of here before these honkys call 5-O on us."

Bishop couldn't afford to have the police called on him because he frequently had arrests warrants that he was dodging.

Finally he was able to pull the lock up, and they left. LaMonica decided right then and there it was probably too embarrassing to go out in public anywhere with Bishop. He just refused to operate by society's rules—whatsoever.

24

THE PROPOSAL

N ow that LaMonica was at Saginaw High full time (mostly) she kept running into Nuggie and her friends in the restroom.

"Has my man tried to call you lately?"

"I told you I never gave him my phone number."

"Oh yeah, that's right."

Nuggie would roll her eyes and then leave out of the bathroom with her friends.

Sometimes it would just be Nuggie's friends in the bathroom.

"Why were you talkin' to Nuggie's man that day?"

"Oh, my goodness. I just went to see what he wanted that day. I have a boyfriend, so I'm not thinking about him."

"Yeah, but why did you talk to him in the first place?"

"Because I didn't know that was her boyfriend. He called *me* over to him, okay!"

"Hmm." They would all roll their eyes as they left out of the bathroom.

No one had threatened her, but they were definitely making things uncomfortable. LaMonica was feeling less and less enthusiastic about attending Saginaw High School. But she kept her word and attend her classes - all but one.

See, even though Mama was now letting Bishop date LaMonica, it didn't deter her from skipping second hour. She was still having a hard time with the fact that she was stuck in gym class. Eventually the principal of Saginaw High called Mama and informed her of LaMonica's continued truancy in second hour.

"Well, please keep me informed day by day. I'll leave work and come get her straight," Mama informed the principal.

Since Mama was allowing Bishop to come over to the house and come pick her up, she asked Bishop about this.

"No, Mrs. Powers, she ain't been skipping with me. I told LaMonica I want her in class," Bishop explained.

They both questioned her in the living room at Mama's house, like two parents working together.

"LaMonica, where are you going when you skip school?" Bishop asked.

"With my friend Jaqueline," LaMonica responded.

"Don't worry, Mrs. Powers, I'm gonna get her straight. Me and LaMonica are going to have a talk."

When LaMonica and Bishop got around the corner to his house on Norman Street, they had that talk. He felt very jealous that LaMonica was out running around in the mornings instead of being in class. *With a pretty girl like her, who knew what she was up to.*

"You need to stay in school, LaMonica. I don't like you out here in the streets when you should be in school, but I'm gonna give you just enough rope to hang yourself. I'm gonna have to try to trust you, but if you mess up, you're gonna end up hanging your own self.

"Besides, don't you remember me telling you how bad it

hurt me when my graduating class rolled down my street celebrating and I didn't get my diploma? I was heartbroken and crying like a baby. Stay in school."

LaMonica whined to Bishop. "But I can't flunk out of school for just missing one class. I just want to miss out on gym because they won't budge. I can't go around looking messed up all day. Hopefully, in a few weeks this class will be up and I can have a new rotating class."

"Look, I know keeping yourself up is important to you, LaMonica. But check this out—I don't know where you at when you out here with Jaqueline, plus I heard she's a hoe. And if I start back picking you up from school, that's gonna upset your Mama and she ain't gonna let us see one another," Bishop explained.

"How about this, wherever me and Jaqueline end up, I'll call you so you know where we are? And I'll talk to you on the phone while I'm there. Then I'll go right back to school after second hour."

"Bet that!" Bishop said. That meant he had come into agreement with LaMonica.

Bishop decided he would need to check up on LaMonica a little bit closer. His brother Alonzo had recently been released from prison. They were riding down the street one day when Bishop told Alonzo-

"Check this out Lonzo I got me a fine honey up at Saginaw High I need to check up on."

"Yeah, I heard Mama and them talking about her. Let's go up there. Besides I wanna see all the little teeny boppers at Saginaw High anyways. They need to know Lonzo is out here. I'm back!"

"Bet that Lonzo. Let's bend this corner and head up there. I can't wait to surprise my woman."

"Dang B, you sound like you in love or something. You ain't lettin' that girl get you strung out, are you?"

Bishop just ignored that question and passed Alonzo a 40 ounce of Old English 800. "Man, here get yo' drank before we bend this corner."

As LaMonica was heading down the stairs from third hour, she heard Bishop calling her name.

"Baby, LaMonica, baby come here."

It surprised LaMonica to see him, and she hugged him. They stood and talked near the stairs' corridor. While they were talking, Alonzo appeared to be high. He was super amped up about being free from prison.

"Yeah! Alonzo out here now y'all. Now what? Now what?" Alonzo said this as he was slapping girls hard on their backsides as they came down the stairs.

Touching girls on their butts against their will was creepy enough to begin with. But he wasn't even subtle with it. Not in the slightest. He was almost like a bully. The way he did it was painful. Each one of them looked shocked and scared. LaMonica felt so guilty for having any part of them going through this. She looked at Alonzo in disgust. *Who did he think he was? They were teenagers, and he was a grown man.* LaMonica hugged Bishop and told him she had to hurry to her next class so he could hurry up and get Alonzo out of there.

Since Mama had asked the principal to inform her in real time when LaMonica was missing from school, she began getting phone calls every morning about LaMonica skipping gym class. Many times Mama would cruise the Saginaw High neighborhood and find her out walking with Jaqueline or other friends and put her in the car and take her back to school. She reported these things back to Bishop so he would know about it (although he already secretly knew anyway).

Mrs. Powers and Bishop's relationship had taken a turn. Suddenly they were working together, or so Mama thought. Bishop saw that Mama was trying to use him like a disciplinarian with LaMonica. Suddenly she was acting like they were on the same team. He saw an opportunity in that.

On his next visit to Mrs. Powers' house to pick up LaMonica, he asked her if they could have a talk. Bishop had a proposal for Mama. Right in front of LaMonica and very much to her surprise he said -

"Mrs. Powers let me and LaMonica get married. If she comes and lives with me, I'll make sure she goes to school and you'd better believe she'll stay there all day if she's living with me."

Bishop went on and explained to Mama how she would have to sign the papers for LaMonica to get married since she was only sixteen. Mama was taken aback but not completely opposed to the idea.

"Give me a little time to work with her and let me see if I can get her straight. If I can't handle her, then I'll go ahead and sign the paper so you can get married."

Bishop was elated. When he and LaMonica were alone, he gave her some instructions.

"Baby, I know I always tell you to go to all your classes and don't skip school, but for the first time ever I'm telling you to mess up! Mess up bad! Skip school the whole day, whatever it takes. That way your mama will sign the paper so we can get married."

LaMonica agreed to do what Bishop said. When she returned to school during homeroom, the principal read another special announcement. He reminded everyone that all students that were now sixteen years old and had a consistent truancy record were now on a list of students to be dropped from the school. Some students had only one time left to skip school. He read over the list of names of those particular students. As he read the list over the loud-speaker, LaMonica's name was on it.

Even after hearing her name read on that list, LaMonica didn't falter in following Bishop's directions. She skipped school again as he had instructed her to. She was promptly dropped from the school and referred to a special dropout program at an alternative school called OIC.

At this point Bishop went to Mama and asked her to sign the marriage papers. Mama didn't keep her word in their agreement. She refused. LaMonica didn't really fret about it, though. Bishop bought them both engagement rings for when they could get married in the future. Even though it was highly irregular for a man to wear one, this was the way he wanted it. The engagement rings were gold bands, and so it appeared that they were married to everyone.

LaMonica entered the OIC alternative school program for students aged sixteen through adults. They had many courses for adults who needed quick job training instead of going to college, and they also offered high school classes for dropouts to complete. The classes were much smaller and easier for LaMonica to handle, and so she didn't mind going. She was excited to go to this new atmosphere.

Of course the boys were trying to holler. She let each one of them know she had a boyfriend and was engaged. Bishop had often warned her that he knew a lot of people and if she **ever** stepped out of line, he would find out about it.

Since OIC was for adults and teens, it was easy for Bishop to not only come up to the school but to come inside as well. He began coming up to the school to her class door, looking more like a parent than a boyfriend. On his first appearance to her class to "check on her" he was wearing a half shirt with holes in it covered in oil. He had been working on his car and came directly up to the school looking like that. He didn't know any of LaMonica's peers in the high school class, but he was very familiar with the adults in adult learning. They were giving each other dap (fist bumping vertically).

The teens in LaMonica's class were dumbfounded when they saw that this was her boyfriend. How could such a pretty girl be with this rough-looking man? Bishop wasn't necessarily ugly. He had a charm in his own way. But he had lived a hard life living on his own, and it showed. At nineteen, he looked more like a man in his late twenties or early thirties. Coming up to the school after working on cars with oil all over his face and clothes only amplified this.

All the teens in LaMonica's class were like her. They wore up-to-date clothes. Even when Bishop wasn't covered in oil during his visits to the school, his clothing was always two decades old. He looked more like LaMonica's parent than her boyfriend. Even the way he spoke and carried himself resonated more with the adult learners in the school than people her age. As a teenager, this was embarrassing for LaMonica. One of the students in her class even remarked, "Man, that dude looks rough. He looks like he be beating your ass."

This was far from the truth. Although Bishop was a bit controlling, he had not put his hands on her.

25

THE FINAL TEST

Mama continued to let Bishop pick LaMonica up because at least she was doing her school work at OIC and not skipping and running away. But unbeknownst to her, Bishop and LaMonica were still in full on "let's make a baby" mode. They were actively having sex without using any protection. After a while Bishop told LaMonica, "Girl, you pregnant. I can feel it."

"Feel it how?" LaMonica asked.

"I can feel it in my left testicle. LaMonica I'm telling you; I just know. I can tell."

Bishop and his family believed in a lot of superstitions, so LaMonica didn't know how seriously she could take this. But she was late having her period, so she thought maybe she would check.

Right before Bishop mentioned this, Mama had become suspicious about LaMonica not having a period. She watched her just *that* close and went through her dirty clothes to check for any signs of a menstruation. When she didn't see any she went off one day.

"How come I haven't seen you have a period around here lately?" Mama asked.

"I did have my period, Mama. I was just extra careful with changing my pads and I washed my own clothes."

"Uh huh. Well, I know one thang you'd better not come up with a baby around here. Because that Bishop ain't nothin' but some trash. You'll end up just like these other women around here if you have a baby with that trash," Mama said harshly.

LaMonica was getting worried now. Missing her period had skipped right over her until Mama began bringing it up. She decided she needed to take a test to find out soon. She had become friendly at school with a heavyset, dark-skinned girl named Tiffany. Tiffany had been telling LaMonica how she had been trying to have a baby and she was going to go take a pregnancy test at the nearby Houghton Jones Clinic on the next lunch hour. LaMonica didn't tell her she and Bishop were planning on making a baby. She just said, "I'll go with you too and take a test just in case."

When LaMonica and Tiffany arrived at the clinic, which was just a short walk away from OIC, most of the staff there seemed to be familiar with Tiffany. Apparently she was a regular who often came in to take a pregnancy test, hoping she would be pregnant. Each and every time her pregnancy test was negative, but she was super hopeful this time. LaMonica wasn't sure. Even though she was actively having unprotected sex with Bishop and had made an agreement with him to have a baby, she wasn't sure if she was doing the right thing.

LaMonica and Tiffany sat in the waiting room. She noticed that the girls who waited on their test results and then came back out quickly had a brown paper bag with them. Tiffany explained that this meant their test was negative. The brown paper bags contained condoms. The girls who were pregnant got ushered into a different room and were there much longer. Tiffany had seen it time and time again. Although she didn't know what was behind door number two (the pregnancy door) because she had never passed the test.

They called Tiffany in first before LaMonica. She went in and came back out with a brown paper bag and told LaMonica her test was of course negative.

Finally, LaMonica was called back. She took the test and went back out to the waiting room to wait on her results. They called her back. The nurse did not hand her a brown paper bag.

"Where's my brown paper bag?" LaMonica asked.

"Oh honey, you will not be needing one of those just yet. We need you to talk with the Nurse Practitioner."

LaMonica went and sat in the Nurse Practitioner's office.

"Your test was positive, hun. You're pregnant. We estimate you to be about six weeks along. Here's a magazine on healthy pregnancies. I see according to your paperwork you're only sixteen years old. I'll need to notify your mother."

LaMonica panicked. She had put her phone number on the application, and now they were going to call Mama.

"Please don't call my mother. She's gonna be so angry with me when I get home if you call and tell her."

"Okay, I won't call her today, LaMonica, but she needs to know. I'll give you a week to tell her. If you haven't told her by then I will have to call myself and inform her you're pregnant. You're a minor and she needs to know. Also you need to get in with a doctor's appointment and get set up on WIC and vitamins for the health of you and your baby."

"Okay, I'll tell her," LaMonica lied.

When LaMonica came out from the office Tiffany was in the waiting room looking for her with excitement. "I don't see you with a brown paper bag. Girl, you were in there for a long time too. You must be pregnant."

"I am," LaMonica said with a bit of anxiety.

"Oh, you're so lucky. I come here every couple of weeks and every time I'm not pregnant. Your baby is gonna be so pretty too."

LaMonica was only half listening to Tiffany. Now that being pregnant was real, she was panicked and didn't know what to do. She certainly didn't want to face Mama. She had to get out of Mama's house before she found out and before the lady from Houghton Jones Clinic called and told her she was pregnant. LaMonica was filled with panic and fear.

She walked back to OIC with Tiffany and then went home from school that day. As soon as LaMonica got there, she asked Mama if she could go to Luchie's house. Maybe Luchie could help her. She would know what to do because she had a baby.

LaMonica began telling Luchie, her mother and her sister Amalia, what the situation was.

"Are you sure you're pregnant, Ma-ma?" Juana (Luchie's mother) asked.

"Yes, Juana. I took a test at the Houghton Jones Clinic. The nurse says I'm six weeks along."

"So what are you gonna do, LaMonica? Because you know Mrs. Powers is gonna be pissed about you having a baby and she can't stand Bishop," Luchie asked.

"Me and Bishop are gonna move in together," LaMonica answered.

"Yeah, but you can't move out of your mom's house legally until you're seventeen," Amalia interjected.

"Luchie found that out from the police the hard way when she tried to run away before she had her baby. Ain't that right Luchie?"

"Yeah, that's right, LaMonica. I'm glad the police kept bringing me back because home was the best place for me, anyway. But if you try to leave your mom's house and live with Bishop and she files a runaway report, they'll just pick you up and make you go back home. You could even end up in Juvenile like I did."

Luchie had gotten in with some terrible people who used her naivete against her to exploit her and lure her into drugs. That's why she kept running away from home. Her situation was totally different from LaMonica's—or so LaMonica thought.

"Man, I gotta go tell Bishop this," LaMonica said.

"He doesn't even know I'm pregnant for sure."

Luchie agreed to walk around the corner to Norman Street so that LaMonica could let Bishop know she was having his baby. After finding out that the law does not allow sixteen-year-olds to move out of their parents' homes without permission, LaMonica asked Luchie and her family if she could move in with them (if she could convince Mama). They all seemed to agree, but the consensus was that they didn't want Mrs. Powers getting upset with them. LaMonica thought maybe she should discuss this with Bishop first when she and Luchie go let him know about her positive pregnancy test.

LaMonica and Luchie walked around the corner to Bishop's house. He was elated to hear that he was going to be a father. He was jumping up and down in the house. At one point he picked LaMonica up, then he directly put her back down. "Oh no, I have to be careful with you. I don't want to hurt the baby."

LaMonica and Luchie told him the information about the law and how she was considering staying with Luchie until she was seventeen. This would mean she would live with Luchie until after the baby was born, because LaMonica wouldn't turn seventeen until the baby was approximately three months old.

"Nawl man. I think we can work around that," Bishop said.

Bishop said he was going to go talk to his brother and his wife. Alonzo was married to a White woman. He had gotten married while he was locked up, which helped him get an early release, and they had their own place. Alonzo's wife, Becky seemed pretty smart, and she had family members who worked for the state of Michigan. Hence they made a plan that Bishop would run over there and LaMonica was going back to Luchie's house to see if she could get Luchie's mom to be her backup plan.

Luchie and LaMonica began walking back to Luchie's house. Just as they were rounding the corner Mama came out of nowhere and pulled up on the side of them. She screeched the car to a halt. You could tell she was angry too.

"LaMonica, get in his car now!" Mrs. Powers shouted.

LaMonica and Luchie looked at each other. *She must know something*, the two of them thought. Mama had a sixth sense for things and she was a super sleuth.

"I think your mom's been by my house, LaMonica. My mom might have told her," Luchie whispered.

"I said now Gal!"

LaMonica got in the car and Mama screeched off. She was racing down the street. Mama always obeyed all the laws because she fancied herself a police officer, so Mama driving like a bat out of hell through the city was new to

LaMonica. She was not showing any signs of slowing down either. This was making LaMonica nervous.

"Mama, where are we going?"

"Don't you worry about it. You just sit back Ms. Powers and make sure you have your seatbelt on."

Oh snap, LaMonica was Ms. Powers today, this must be really bad.

"You think I'm a fool around here, LaMonica. Well, I ain't no fool," Mama continued.

"Mama, I don't think you're a fool. Where are we going?"

"Yeah, you do. You think everybody's crazy but you. But I ain't crazy LaMonica. I wasn't born yesterday," Mama said as she raced through the east side of Saginaw.

LaMonica wasn't sure where they were going until they got nearer and nearer to Bishop's mother's house. They pulled up in Anna's driveway.

"Mama, why are we here? Let's go."

Mama completely ignored LaMonica and jumped out of the car and began beating on Anna's door like she was the police. Anna came running to the door, thinking it was an emergency. She had met Mrs. Powers before when she had come over to complain about Bishop and LaMonica not going on real dates and to also complain about them exchanging clothes with one another, which Mrs. Powers did not approve of because she purchased LaMonica's clothing. Anna had tried to explain to Mrs. Powers at the time that Bishop was a nineteen-year-old adult, and she didn't control what he did. But she explained to Mrs. Powers that boyfriends and girlfriends wore each other's clothes all the time, especially at LaMonica and Bishop's age. She could tell Mrs. Powers was from the old way and didn't know anything about these things.

LaMonica thought she'd better go to the door and see what was going on.

Anna opened the door and when she saw it was Mrs. Powers and LaMonica standing behind her looking nervous she asked, "What's going on? I thought the police were out here or something."

Mrs. Powers was attempting to push her way into Anna's house through the front door without even being let in.

"Yeah, I would like to talk to you," she said with the meanest attitude ever.

Anna was a little guarded, to say the least, with the way Mrs. Powers was seeking to take control at her door. Later, she and Bishop would describe it as bo-guarding.

"Talk to me about what?"

"About how your son has **ruined** my daughter's life," she loudly exclaimed.

Mrs. Powers was still pushing her way through the door while saying this. Anna just went ahead and stepped aside. She gave Mrs. Powers respect because of her age and because she was obviously upset about something serious.

"Okay, well, I'm just getting home from work, Mrs. Powers. Come on in, I guess, while I go take off these lounge clothes and put on something proper. Y'all go ahead and have a seat on the couch," Anna sweetly said. She was trained in de-escalating situations, and so she tried to use that in this case.

Mrs. Powers and LaMonica sat in the living room on the couch. Anna quickly emerged from the bedroom and sat down opposite of LaMonica and Mrs. Powers on the other couch. She was on the edge of her seat.

"Please tell me what is going on, Mrs. Powers?"

"LaMonica is pregnant. I told her and Bishop not to come up here with no baby. I even told him he could date her as long as he used rubbers. Now LaMonica ain't got no business having no baby."

Anna's face was shocked. Her light skin turned red. This threw her. She was upset with Bishop for being irresponsible, but secretly happy she was going to be a grandmother again at the same time (Alonzo had an older child). But she couldn't let on, especially with how upset Mrs. Powers was.

Mrs. Powers began bashing Bishop right away, and Anna just let her. "Bishop is running around here having sex with LaMonica without protection and he ain't got no job. He's not ready to be a father. He pulls up in my driveway, playing that loud music. And all he does is rip and run the streets." Mama wanted to call him a bum and really tell Anna the trash that she thought he was, but thought that might be going too far with his own mother.

"Well, Bishop *is* really immature. I can agree with you on that, Mrs. Powers. I don't know why these two weren't using protection in the first place. Mrs. Powers, you best believe me I'm going to be talking to my son and he's going to need to get himself a job instead of all that riding up and down the streets doing whatever he's doing. He has responsibilities now. He's got a baby to take care of."

"Oh, she ain't keeping it," Mama declared. "I'm taking LaMonica to have an abortion."

"Now hold on Mrs. Powers," Anna's voice had a serious tone but not loud. "I don't believe in abortions. No ma'am. My family and I we don't believe in that."

LaMonica was glad that Anna had said that, but at the same time it was crazy how the two of them were going back and forth deciding what she was going to do with *her* life.

"Oh, she's having that abortion," Mama stated again.

"Now listen Mrs. Powers I will do all I can to help support Bishop taking care of his baby and to help support

LaMonica with their new baby when it comes, but I will not support helping her get an abortion. Absolutely not!"

Anna was very clear on her stance on the situation and with that she stood up indicating that it was time for Mrs. Powers to go.

"Well, I was just letting you know. From this point forward, I don't want your son anywhere near my daughter. She will not be going out with him anymore and she will be getting an abortion."

"Good day, Mrs. Powers," is all Anna could respectfully say.

LaMonica knew there was no way she was getting an abortion, but she wasn't about to argue with Mama because you could tell her blood pressure was up. Her eyes were popping out again and her cheeks were shaking. She was making decisions and bo- guarding into people's houses like it was nothing. Nawl Mama was in full on angry mode, so she just sat quietly.

Honestly, the whole thing made LaMonica feel frazzled because she was thrown into the situation without being able to prepare her thoughts when Mama never told her where they were going. It was like her shocked senses wouldn't allow her to respond. She stayed on guard at Anna's house the whole time to make sure Mama didn't take things too out of hand.

Riding home, LaMonica wished she had had something quick witted to say back to Mama against the abortion when Anna was present to be on her side. Now she had all kinds of comebacks, but she didn't dare say them out loud to Mama while she was in this state of anger.

When Mama said she didn't want Bishop around LaMonica because he had gotten her pregnant, she meant that. She took every avenue possible to make that happen.

First she went up to OIC and spoke with the offices and made sure that they understood who Bishop was and what he looked like. He was under no circumstances to be let in that building or near her classes.

Next she commenced to telling Luchie, Olivia and Kristina everything she knew or any negative theories she had about Bishop. The main one being that he was just using LaMonica. She told not only them but their parents also about every bad thing she had observed or ever heard about Bishop, including rumors, so they would be on her side. Honestly, this wasn't hard to do because they already had their own reservations about him, anyway.

After Mama got done everyone who knew LaMonica thought she was a downright fool to be with Bishop and told her as much. So now if LaMonica was going to be with him, she was almost going to have to choose between her friends and him. Mama felt like she was fighting for LaMonica's future and her life, so she showed no mercy in this situation.

The next phase in Mama's plan was to get LaMonica to have an abortion before it was too late. She asked her repeatedly at home to have an abortion. Each time, there was no convincing her. LaMonica always answered with a resounding, "NO! I'm not killing my baby. How can you ask me that?"

"LaMonica right now it's not even a baby, it's just a ball of blood. That's why I'm trying to take you to have an abortion before it's too late."

This sounded like faulty science to LaMonica. Deep in her heart she knew it was a baby, and that God would not be pleased with her for killing a baby.

LaMonica was being so stubborn that Mrs. Powers set up a meeting with her favorite counselor and asked her if there was any way she could force LaMonica against her will to have an abortion since she was underage.

"No, Mrs. Powers, that's the choice of the teen. She has rights. But with all this going on with LaMonica, it would probably be a good idea for you to schedule her an appointment to come and see me."

LaMonica went in to see her favorite counselor. She asked her pointedly what would she do in her situation? The counselor told her what Mama had tried to do behind the scenes with forcing her to get an abortion and how that was not legal and could not happen. But she also gave her opinion since she asked.

"Honestly knowing what I know now as an adult, I would get the abortion."

That was not what LaMonica wanted or was expecting to hear. She definitely didn't agree with that, but she thanked the counselor for being honest with her.

Soon after that Mama informed LaMonica that Luchie and her family wanted to see her. LaMonica headed over to Luchie's house down the street in the car with Mama. They were all seated at the round table Luchie, her sister Amalia, and Luchie's mother Juana. This was obviously some sort of intervention. Mama had convinced them to all be on her side. One by one they went around the table telling LaMonica why she should have an abortion. LaMonica couldn't believe that Luchie had switched up like this.

"Luchie, you have a baby yourself. How can you say this?"

"Exactly LaMonica and that's why I can tell you it's hard. You see, I never go anywhere. All my money goes on my child. All my time goes to her too. No one babysits for me because it's my responsibility. I'm the one who got pregnant. If you have this baby, you can probably say goodbye to all those name brand clothes Mrs. Powers buys you. All that money will now go on the baby. Listen LaMonica you're only a few weeks you can still get an abortion and graduate and go to college. Then later have a baby in your twenties if you still want to."

Juana began speaking to LaMonica. "Yeah, look at Amalia, Ma-ma. She's stuck in the house with these kids. And only every blue moon does she get a break, when she can pay a babysitter. Once you start having one, it's easy to have more LaMonica. Just listen to your mom."

"Don't get me wrong LaMonica I love my kids and I wouldn't trade them for the world. But if I would've thought things through, I would have waited and had them later. Mrs. Powers is just asking you to wait till later," Amalia explained.

"But you can't just kill one kid and then wait and trade it for having another one later. That's not right," LaMonica passionately said.

She felt so betrayed by everybody. Luchie and them were her peoples. This was her family. Her familia. Then Luchie got real serious and dealt the final blow.

"Listen, LaMonica! You don't leave your mom's house to go and get on welfare with some dude. **Don't you understand that?!**"

LaMonica couldn't believe they had said this in front of Mama. Everybody was against her. Nobody was for her keeping her baby except Bishop. It felt like it was just him and her against the world, and she wasn't even allowed to see him. So in truth, it was just her against the whole world.

They didn't convince her, so she and Mama went home. But Mama didn't let up. She knew this was a race against time. LaMonica was advancing in weeks and she couldn't let her get too far along before it was too late to have the abortion, so she brought it up every single day and her methods got more and more intense.

LaMonica had no one. Birdie had moved out of town with her brothers Chuck and Malcolm so she couldn't even talk to them about this. All of her friends were on Mama's side. There was no one.

Finally Mama had one more person to try to talk some sense into LaMonica, her father.

One day Mama says, "LaMonica your daddy wants to talk to you."

LaMonica and Mama headed over to Daddy's house. His girlfriend Linda was home. The baby was there too. She was now one year old. It was apparent right away that Mama had already spoken with Daddy about this issue.

"Chuck, LaMonica doesn't need no baby. She needs to finish school so she can go to college. That's why she needs to go on ahead and have this abortion."

"I agree with Mrs. Powers," Daddy said, facing LaMonica.

"And from what I hear, this dude ain't no count. He ain't nobody you should be having a baby with anyway. You need to go ahead and have this abortion LaMonica," Daddy said firmly.

LaMonica had never, ever disagreed with Daddy in her life. Well, not for all the time that Mama had allowed her to see him. Anything he would ask her to do, she would do. But this—this she just couldn't do. And unlike the time when she was at Anna's house, she found her words.

"Look, killing a baby is wrong. No matter what any of you say. The only one who is gonna have to stand and face God for that would be me. And I'm not doing it! I'm not killing my baby!"

Linda's eyes got big. She couldn't believe that LaMonica

had stood up to her daddy like that. Secretly she was happy, but she wasn't going to say anything to back her up in front of him.

"I'm going to tell you just one last time LaMonica - either you have an abortion or you ain't my daughter. I won't have nothin' to do with you."

LaMonica couldn't believe he had said this. She looked at him with tears streaming down her face and she said, "I'm not having no abortion, Daddy."

Daddy meant what he said. That was the end of him speaking to LaMonica.

"Mrs. Powers, get her out of my house! She ain't nothing to me from this point forward."

Mama and LaMonica backed out of Daddy's driveway with her in the passenger seat of Mama's car, completely heartbroken. Everybody had turned against her, even Daddy at this point.

LaMonica favored Chuck so much over her, that Mrs. Powers was almost glad to see him hurt her feelings. At least now she knew she was all that she really had.

Mama gave up trying to convince LaMonica to have an abortion directly. As the weeks passed instead, she went a different route. She called LaMonica's General Practitioner Doctor and told him that LaMonica was pregnant. Because of LaMonica's special circumstance with her heart condition, according to Mama, they said special measures would have to be put in place. And she was definitely a high-risk pregnancy, meaning there was a high-risk to her own safety to have this baby. Mama definitely intensified her words when she told LaMonica this information, too.

"I talked to your doctors and all the people in his office, because this is such a special circumstance. They said they've never had a patient with your heart condition have a baby before. They also said they don't know what they're gonna have to do. They may have to freeze your heart. You are a high-risk pregnancy, which means you have a higher likelihood rate of something happening to you or the baby if you continue this pregnancy. I just thought you should know what you are getting into. You could die having this baby."

Now **this** got to LaMonica because she carried a little bit of Daddy's anxiety. If you really wanted to stop her from doing something you could scare her with death. Mama probably knew it too.

Now, for the first time, LaMonica actually seriously considered it. One day when Mama was at work and Ms. Demona was busy with her boyfriend, LaMonica snuck out of the house around the corner to Bishop's. She told him what Mama had said about the doctor's message.

"Do you think I should consider having an abortion for my health? My mama says I could die."

"You're not gonna die! Your mama is just trying to scare you. If you do that mess I'll never speak to you again."

LaMonica spent a short time with Bishop and then hurried home before anyone knew she was missing. She had a lot to consider. Was she willing to put her life on the line? Will she trust God? And could she go without any family or friends through this process?

Order Mixed Out: Book Two Now

MIXED OUT

The Mixed Girl Series

Book Two

LAMONIQUE MAC

SIGN UP FOR MY AUTHOR NEWSLETTER

Be the first to learn about LaMonique Mac's new releases and receive exclusive content for fiction readers.

www.authorlamoniquemac.com

I hope you enjoyed reading this book as much as I enjoyed writing it. If you did, I'd sincerely appreciate a review on your favorite book retailer's website, Goodreads, and Book-Bub. Reviews are crucial for any author, and even just a line or two can make a huge difference.

ACKNOWLEDGMENTS

Thank you to my husband, Terry Cooper, who was there for me while I dug through the recesses of my soul to write this book. Thank you for being there to give me advice and to bounce ideas off of as my best friend. Thank you for holding me and telling me I am a beautiful worthwhile person after hearing some of the tormenting tales of my childhood. And thank you for backing me and believing in my God given writing talent.

Thank you to my son, Junior, for your sacrifices in being a little bit quieter while I penned this novel. Thank you for listening while I shared.

Thank you to my readers. I pray this series enlightens you to the things God wants to share upon your hearts.

ABOUT THE AUTHOR

LaMonique Mac is an Author, Writing Coach and Publisher. She writes in the genres of Christian, Young Adult and Nonfiction. She's based in "Roll Tide" country Alabama with her family.

The books she has written and published are known for having a southern flair.

She can be spotted coaching new authors on how to write, edit, and publish on YouTube at Author LaMonique Mac.

instagram.com/authorlamoniquemac

facebook.com/lamoniquemac

twitter.com/LamoniqueMac

Made in the USA
Coppell, TX
18 May 2022

77929412R00134